THERE WERE EIGHT ITEMS ON Coke McDonald's To
Do list on June 25. But having his body lowered into a
vat of boiling oil was not one of them.

SING HAPPY BIRTHDAY TO PEP was on the list.

DO A DUMP was on the list.

WASH MY CLOTHES was on the list.

CLEAN UP MY STUFF was on the list.

But nothing about being lowered into a vat of boiling oil.

And yet, oddly enough, having his body lowered
into a vat of boiling oil—along with his sister, Pepsi—
was the *one* thing that Coke McDonald was actually
going To Do on June 25.

DAN GUTMAN

THE GENIUS FILES

NEVER SAY GENIUS

HARPER

An Imprint of HarperCollinsPublishers

To Barbara Lalicki, Laura Arnold,
Elyse Marshall, and all the folks at HarperCollins,
who have been so supportive.

The Genius Files #2: Never Say Genius
Copyright © 2012 by Dan Gutman
information address HarperCollins Children's Books,
a division of HarperCollins Publishers,
10 East 53rd Street, New York, NY 10022.
www.harpercollinschildrens.com

Library of Congress Cataloging-in-Publication Data
Gutman, Dan.
Never say genius / Dan Gutman. — 1st ed.
    p. cm. — (The Genius Files ; #2)
Summary: As their cross-country journey with their parents
continues through the midwest, twins Coke and Pepsi, now
thirteen, again face strange assassins at such places as the first
McDonald's restaurant and Cedar Point amusement park.
  ISBN 978-0-06-182769-3 (pbk.)
[1. Adventure and adventurers—Fiction. 2. Genius—Fiction.
3. Brothers and sisters—Fiction. 4. Twins—Fiction. 5. Assassins—
Fiction. 6. Recreational vehicles—Fiction. 7. Family life—Fiction.]
I. Title.
PZ7.G9846Nev 2012   2011019363
[Fic]—dc23

Art and typography by Erin Fitzsimmons
12 13 14 15 16   CG/BR   10 9 8 7 6 5 4 3 2 1
❖
First paperback edition, 2013

"Every bad thing that happens in the world
is good for somebody."
—*Nobody said this. But somebody should have.*

Thanks to Jim Beard, Esther Goldenberg, Karen and Katie Jergensen, Anne Kalkowski, Mary Kittrell, Jennifer and Jabin Mallory, Sue Marchbanks, Shelley Riskin, Kelly Salgado, Fred Valentini, and Nina Wallace. And a special thank-you to Google Maps and Roadside America.com, without which this book could not have been written.

Cont

ents

To the Reader . . .
All the places mentioned in this book are real. You
can visit them. You *should* visit them!

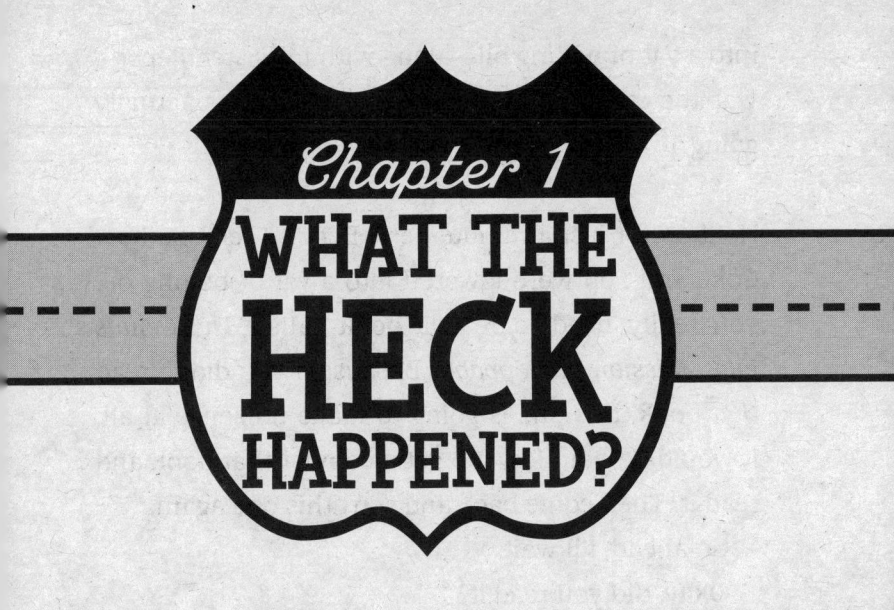

Chapter 1
WHAT THE HECK HAPPENED?

There were eight items on Coke McDonald's To Do list on June 25. But having his body lowered into a vat of boiling oil was not one of them.

SING HAPPY BIRTHDAY TO PEP was on the list.

DO A DUMP was on the list.

WASH MY CLOTHES was on the list.

CLEAN UP MY STUFF was on the list.

But nothing about being lowered into a vat of boiling oil.

And yet, oddly enough, having his body lowered

into a vat of boiling oil—along with his sister, Pepsi—was the *one* thing that Coke McDonald was actually going To Do on June 25.

🦌

Hold on for just a minute here. Before I tell you how Coke and Pep were lowered into a vat of boiling oil, you really need to read a book called *The Genius Files: Mission Unstoppable*. Because if you didn't read *that* book, this one is going to make no sense at all. It would be pointless. So get a copy of that book and read it. Then come back and start this one again.

Go ahead, I'll wait.

Okay, did you read it?

Liar!

What do you want me to do, read it *to* you? You lazy bum! If you don't want to read *The Genius Files: Mission Unstoppable*, get the audio book. If you're *really* lazy, you can just Google it and read the summary online. What do I have to do, tuck you into bed at night too? Sheesh. I'm busy. What's the matter with you kids today?

Fine, don't read *The Genius Files: Mission Unstoppable*. See if I care. Basically, this is what happened. . . .

(Deep breath)

Coke and Pep—they're twins—were walking home from their school in California when a mysterious guy wearing a bowler hat started chasing them in a golf cart. Some lady wearing all red named Mya appeared out of nowhere and threw an exploding Frisbee grenade to take out the bowler dude. But Coke and Pep had to jump off a cliff after Mya got hit in the neck by a tranquilizer dart shot by another mysterious bowler dude (the first guy's brother) riding a golf cart. Luckily, Mya had given the twins wingsuits to wear, so they could jump off the cliff, fly through the air, and land safely on the beach.

(Deep breath)

Following me so far? Good.

You see, what Coke and Pep didn't realize was that they had been recruited to be part of a secret government program run by the eccentric Dr. Herman Warsaw. He's a genius inventor who had decided that the grown-ups of the world were hopeless. The only way to solve our problems would be to use the skills of the smartest kids in America. He called his program—wait for it—"The Genius Files." As a reward for being a part of this dangerous program, the kids were promised a million dollars when they turned twenty-one.

Unfortunately, it didn't look like Coke and Pep would ever reach that birthday, because someone was trying very hard to kill them. The next day at school, they were locked in the detention room and almost burned alive when the school was set on fire. The fire was set by their germ-phobic health teacher, Mrs. Higgins, who turned out to be an evil psychopath. Fortunately, the twins were rescued by the obese deaf/mute janitor Bones, who turned out to be skinny and quite talkative after he removed his fat suit.

Bones was part of The Genius Files team (as was Mya). To track the McDonald twins' every move, he used a staple gun to implant tiny GPS devices designed by Dr. Warsaw in their skulls.

(Deep breath)

Still with me? Great!

The next day the twins started on a cross-country summer RV trip with their clueless parents, who must never learn about The Genius Files program. Along the way to their Aunt Judy's wedding in Washington, D.C., Coke and Pep . . .

- Watched a building blow up moments after they left it.
- Were pushed into a ditch at the top of a singing sand dune in Nevada and left to die there.
- Witnessed their dad go through his midlife crisis by seeing how fast he could drive the RV on the Bonneville Salt Flats in Utah.

- Visited lots of oddball tourist destinations (a museum devoted to Pez dispensers, the National Yo-Yo Museum, the largest ball of twine in the world, and the *second* largest ball of twine in the world), because their mom runs a popular website called *Amazing but True*.
- Were thrown into a giant vat of SPAM in Minnesota.
- Dropped five days' worth of human waste on the head of Mrs. Higgins (their germ-phobic, psychopath health teacher, remember).
- Were given a series of increasingly difficult secret messages, which they had to decipher.
- Had a climactic confrontation with the person who had been trying to kill them.

In the end, guess who was trying to kill Coke and Pep the whole time? It was Dr. Warsaw, the inventor of The Genius Files. Ha! Who'd a thunk it?

(Deep breath)

Whew! Let's see *you* try to sum up a 304-page book in just three breaths.

The story really wasn't nearly as complicated as it sounds . . . *if* you read *The Genius Files: Mission Unstoppable*. It just seems that way when you try to compress a lot of stuff into a few paragraphs.

Anyway, that's basically what happened in the first book. Now you don't.have to read it yourself. You could even write a book report on it if you wanted to.

Our new story begins in Spring Green, Wisconsin, where *Mission Unstoppable* left off. If you'd like to follow the McDonalds on their trip east to Washington, it's easy. Get on the internet and go to Google Maps (http://maps.google.com/), MapQuest (www.mapquest.com), Rand McNally (www.randmcnally.com) or whatever navigation website you like best.

Go ahead, I'll wait.

Okay, now type in Spring Green, Wisconsin, and click SEARCH MAPS. Click the little + or – sign on the screen to zoom out until you get a sense of where the twins are. See it? That's the starting point.

Now that we've gotten all that preliminary non-sense out of the way, let's get to the cool part—the part where Coke and Pep get lowered into a vat of boiling oil. . . .

Chapter 2
YOU WANT
FRIES
WITH THAT?

Happy birthday to you . . .

It was June 25. The McDonald family (Coke, Pep, their mom, Bridget, and dad, Dr. Benjamin McDonald) were sitting in the RV in the parking lot of The House on the Rock. Mrs. McDonald had baked a little cake in the microwave oven. Dr. McDonald stuck thirteen candles in it and lit them. That's the problem with getting older—at some point your birthday cake becomes a fire hazard.

"Can you believe we have a couple of teenagers on our hands, Ben?" asked Mrs. McDonald, shaking her head at the wonder of it all.

"Do you remember the day they were born?" he replied (as if she could ever forget). "I held each of them in my arms like a couple of footballs. I remember it like it was yesterday. And now look at them."

Coke and Pep sat in the backseat, silent. They were still stunned after what had happened to them at The House on the Rock. Just minutes earlier, they had been captured by Dr. Warsaw in The Infinity Room, a pointy extension that hung off the house like the beak of a huge bird. Dr. Warsaw had given them a choice: die by electric shock from the wireless iJolt he had invented, or plummet one hundred fifty feet to their deaths. They chose neither. Instead, Pep knocked the iJolt out of his hands with a Frisbee, and Coke used his famous Inflictor karate move to kick Dr. Warsaw out of The Infinity Room and to his virtually certain death. It would be awhile before the twins would be ready to return to anything resembling normal.

"It's time for your birthday presents!" Mrs. McDonald announced.

"Yay!"

A while was over. The twins, being of short attention span (like most thirteen-year-olds) instantly forgot all about Dr. Warsaw and their ordeal at The House on the Rock.

"What did you get us?" Pep asked anxiously, clapping her hands together.

"Just a little souvenir to help you remember our fun time in Wisconsin," Dr. McDonald told them. With that, he presented them with a framed photo of The Infinity Room.

Coke gulped and Pep lurched backward in her seat involuntarily. Somebody had *died* at The Infinity Room. And it had almost been *them*. They certainly didn't need a constant reminder hanging on the wall.

"But that's not all!" said Mrs. McDonald, in her best infomercial voice.

She presented each of the twins with a little plastic bag filled with what appeared to be those Styrofoam peanuts that are used to pack boxes.

"What is it?" Pep asked.

"Cheese curds!" Mrs. McDonald exclaimed. "You

can only get them in Wisconsin. Go ahead, taste one. When you bite into them, they squeak."

"We also got you some genuine Wisconsin Cheeseheads," Dr. McDonald added, pulling the big goofy yellow hats out of a bag and handing one to each twin. "Cool, huh?"

"It's awesome, Dad," Pep said semi-sarcastically as she put on her Cheesehead.

"We knew you'd like them," said Dr. McDonald.

He pulled out of the parking lot and into the first gas station on the road to fill the tank of the RV. Then he merged onto Route 14 East heading out of Spring Green. Dr. McDonald had attended graduate school at the University of Wisconsin and knew the area well. Soon they were in the country, passing by the rolling hills and dairy farms of southern Wisconsin.

"Look, a cow!" Pep hollered.

"Big wow," Coke said. "What, you never saw a cow before?"

"Be nice to your sister," warned Dr. McDonald.

"It's Wisconsin!" Coke said. "Do you have any idea how many cows they have in Wisconsin?"

"I give up," Pep admitted. "How many?"

"One point two million," Coke said.

There was no point in arguing with him. Coke had a photographic memory. He could remember virtually anything he ever saw, touched, heard, smelled, or tasted. And one day, several years earlier, he happened to be reading the back of a milk carton that said there were 1.2 million cows in Wisconsin. Of course, there could be more cows now, or less. But at some point in time, there were definitely 1.2 million cows in Wisconsin.

"Hey, speaking of cows," Dr. McDonald said, "do you know what kind of milk comes from a forgetful cow?"

"What kind?" everybody asked.

"Milk of amnesia!"

"Lame, Dad," Coke said.

Actually, Coke thought his father's joke was minorly funny. But it's not cool to laugh at your parents' jokes, as you well know.

It seemed like there were dairy farms everywhere. Wisconsin is the cheese capital of the world. Coke put on his Cheesehead to get into the spirit of it. Pep munched on cheese curds, which actually did squeak when she bit into them, and they were also delicious.

"The people in Wisconsin probably put cheese on their cornflakes," Coke commented as he looked out the window.

"Cheese is a funny word," said Pep. "Isn't it odd that we say 'cheese' when we take a picture?"

"Everybody does that, doofus," Coke said.

"Don't call your sister a doofus," said Mrs. McDonald. "It's not nice."

"But why do we say 'cheese' when we take a picture?" Pep asked.

"Probably because it forces people to smile," Dr. McDonald said. "You can't say 'cheese' without smiling."

"Well, you can't say 'disease' without smiling either," Coke pointed out. "Why don't people say 'disease' when they're getting their pictures taken?"

"Well, everybody likes cheese, and *nobody* likes disease," said Mrs. McDonald.

"Doctors like disease," Coke said. "If we didn't have diseases, all the doctors would be out of a job. We wouldn't even need doctors anymore. So it's actually in a doctor's interest for there to be lots of people with diseases. If all those people were suddenly cured, it would be a disaster for the medical industry."

Everybody thought about that for a few minutes.

"With that logic," Pep said, "if cars never broke down, all the mechanics would be out of jobs."

"That's true," Coke agreed.

"If there were no arguments," said Dr. McDonald, "we wouldn't need lawyers."

"I guess every bad thing that happens in the world is good for *somebody*," said Mrs. McDonald. "Sometimes good things can be bad things. And sometimes bad things can be good things."

Everybody chewed on that as they drove past the barns and silos that dotted the Wisconsin countryside. The twins were happy and relaxed for the first time since school had let out. Their long nightmare was finally over. They wouldn't have to worry about Dr. Warsaw or Mrs. Higgins or any of those bowler dude psychos who had been trying to kill them. Now they could enjoy the rest of their trip to Aunt Judy's wedding in Washington. It was like a great weight had been lifted off their shoulders.

They had no idea that in a matter of hours, they would be hearing the sizzle of boiling oil as it splattered against their skin.

Mrs. McDonald fiddled with her portable GPS to find out that it is 885 miles from Spring Green, Wisconsin, to Washington, D.C.—almost sixteen hours of straight driving. That is, if you were going to do the whole trip without stopping, which would be crazy. The plan was for them to stay overnight in Chicago and Cleveland, and

also a few other smaller towns along the way.

"We have nine days to get to Washington for Aunt Judy's wedding on the Fourth of July," she announced. "So there's plenty of time to stop off along the way and see some cool sights."

Mrs. McDonald had not seen her sister Judy in ten years, ever since they'd had an argument about a boy Judy was dating. But that was ancient history now, and she was excited and a little nervous about seeing her sister again.

"You're not going to force us to go see the largest cow in the world and stuff like that, are you Mom?" asked Coke.

"I promise," Mrs. McDonald said. "No giant cows."

The McDonalds had been driving for less than an hour on Route 14 when they entered the town of Middleton, Wisconsin, not far from Lake Mendota.

"Stop the RV, Ben!" Mrs. McDonald suddenly shouted.

Dr. McDonald was getting used to these sudden exclamations from his wife. He stomped on the brake and the RV screeched to a halt, almost

Go to Google Maps (http://maps.google .com/).

Click Get Directions.

In the A box, type Spring Green WI.

In the B box, type Middleton WI.

Click Get Directions.

getting rear-ended by the Toyota Camry behind it.

"What is it?" Dr. McDonald said angrily.

There was a sign at the side of the road. . . .

Visit
the National Mustard
Museum

"No!" Coke moaned. "You gotta be kidding me! We already went to the Pez museum. We went to the yo-yo museum. And now *this*. Do we *have* to go? I *hate* mustard."

"Aren't there any giant cows around for us to look at?" asked Pep.

"We're right here!" Mrs. McDonald said. "We *have* to go. If we didn't go, I would spend the rest of my life regretting that I was in Middleton, Wisconsin, and didn't visit the National Mustard Museum. This will be *perfect* for *Amazing but True!*"

Three pairs of eyes rolled. There was no arguing with Mrs. Bridget McDonald when she decided to do something. And she was right. The oddballs who read her website every day would *love* to learn about a museum devoted to mustard.

Dr. McDonald just sighed and drove to the center

of Middleton, where Pep spotted a big sign over a storefront. . . .

As soon as they walked into the museum, their eyes were assaulted by five thousand jars, bottles, and tubes of mustard from all fifty states and more than sixty countries. Polish mustard. Chinese mustard. Australian Outback mustard. There were also antique mustard pots, mustard tins, vintage mustard advertisements, and other assorted mustard memorabilia.

Dr. McDonald shook his head. As a respected history professor and author of *The Impact of Coal on the Industrial Revolution*, he was mystified by the fact that his research grant applications were frequently turned down, but somehow people managed to get funding to build museums devoted to hot dog condiments. He could have spent his summer researching his next book, but instead he was about to waste his money buying jars of mustard in a museum gift shop. Life wasn't fair.

Mrs. McDonald got to work, snapping photos for her website and interviewing strolling mustard lovers about their personal mustard memories. She threw herself into her work, which was why her website was so successful. Even though she didn't personally love mustard, she filled out a form to join the Mustard of the Month Club. So every month for a year, she would receive a new jar of mustard.

"Will you folks be here the first Saturday in August?" asked the man behind the cash register.

"No, we're on our way to my sister's wedding in Washington," replied Mrs. McDonald. "I haven't seen her in ten years."

"Too bad," the guy said. "The first Saturday in August is National Mustard Day. We have a lot of festivities planned. . . ."

Coke and Pep looked at each other and mouthed the words, "Let's get out of here."

When they finally did get out of there, Mrs. McDonald was carrying a large shopping bag.

"I couldn't resist," she told the twins. "I bought you another birthday present."

"Let me guess," Coke said. "A jar of mustard?"

"Of course not!" Mrs. McDonald said. "I know you don't like mustard. Go ahead. Open it."

Coke opened the bag. Inside was a toilet seat, with these words printed on it:

POUPON U

"Get it?" Mrs. McDonald said. "Poupon is a kind of mustard."

"We get it, Mom," Pep said. "Can we go now?"

Coke and Pep had no idea what they were going to do with a Poupon U toilet seat, but they made sure to thank their mother and tell her it was just what they always wanted. You should always accept gifts from loved ones graciously, even if somebody has just given you the dumbest thing in the world.

The RV passed by Madison, the capital of Wisconsin. In the backseat, the twins amused themselves with crossword puzzles and playing cards, blissfully ignorant of the fact that soon they would be lowered into a vat of boiling oil. But you, fortunate reader, know it's coming and

Go to Google Maps (http://maps.google.com/).

Click Get Directions.

In the A box, type Middleton WI.

In the B box, type Fort Atkinson WI.

Click Get Directions.

are probably wondering when that exciting event will happen. Patience. And no skipping ahead!

Dr. McDonald was taking the scenic route, staying off the interstate highway, and enjoying the view. Less than an hour from the Mustard Museum, the RV entered the town of Fort Atkinson and rolled to a stop in the south side of the downtown area outside the Hoard Historical Museum.

"Why are we stopping *here*?" Pep asked, annoyance in her voice.

"Because this is the National Dairy Shrine Visitor's Center," Mrs. McDonald informed her.

"Dairy Shrine?" the twins said together.

And so it was, a shrine to all things dairy. The place was jam-packed with antique milking machines, a dog-powered butter churn, and even Elsie the Cow's original blanket. Mrs. McDonald took notes for *Amazing but True*, while Dr. McDonald examined the dioramas of pioneer dairy life. The twins walked around, searching desperately for an exit sign.

"Look, kids," Mrs. McDonald said enthusiastically. "The National Dairy Hall of Fame!"

On the "Wall of Pioneers" were Harvey D. Thatcher (inventor of the glass milk bottle), Arthur Baer ("World Authority on Ice Cream"), and Thorkeld "Tom" Knudsen (the developer of half-and-half).

"This place is a snooze fest," Coke whispered to his sister.

"They don't even have a cool gift shop," Pep replied as she leafed through the only book for sale, *A History of Dairy Marketing in America*.

The twins would not have been so snarky if they had any idea that they would soon be dropped into a vat of boiling oil. But as you well know, they were clueless.

Thankfully, the McDonalds did not spend much time at the Dairy Shrine and were soon heading south and east on Route 12. In about an hour, they passed a sign . . .

"Woo-hoo!" Coke hollered. "Did you know that Illinois is called 'The Land of Lincoln' even though Abraham Lincoln was born in Kentucky?"

"Thank you, Mr. Know-It-All," muttered Pep, who long ago had grown tired of her brother's encyclopedic memory. "Are we going to stop soon? I'm getting hungry."

"Soon, honey," Mrs. McDonald said. "I know the perfect place to stop for dinner."

"Where? Where?" the kids asked.

"You'll see."

The twins would have to remain in suspense for almost an hour, as they continued on Route 12 south and east through Illinois. Eventually they entered the town of Des Plaines, which is twenty miles outside of Chicago. Dr. McDonald took a right fork onto Lee Street and passed a motel, and then the familiar yellow arches came into view. He pulled into the McDonald's parking lot.

"Here it is!" Mrs. McDonald announced.

"Fifteen cents for a burger!" Dr. McDonald exclaimed. "That's a good deal!"

"What?" Pep asked. "It's a McDonald's. They have

Go to Google Maps (http://maps.google.com/).

Click Get Directions.

In the A box, type Fort Atkinson WI.

In the B box, type Des Plaines IL.

Click Get Directions.

these *everywhere.*"

"We drove an hour just to go to McDonald's?" asked Coke.

"Oh, it's not just *any* McDonald's," Mrs. McDonald told them. "This is the *first* McDonald's!"

"The first *ever*?" asked Pep as she got out of the RV. She was still wearing her Cheesehead.

Indeed it was. At this precise location—400 North Lee Street, Des Plaines, Illinois—the first McDonald's opened on April 15, 1955. It was torn down in 1984, but a replica was built on the spot, sort of a museum to McDonald's. Across the street was a modern McDonald's restaurant.

"So this is where the decline of our civilization began," said Dr. McDonald. "Chain restaurants, cheap, bland, standardized food, wasteful packaging, rampant obesity, the end of home cooking . . ."

"Don't be such a downer, Dad!" said Coke. "This is sacred ground. This is where Happy Meals began! And Ronald McDonald. The Big Mac. Golden arches. Egg McMuffins. Supersizing. Extra Value Meals . . ."

"The Whopper," added Pepsi.

"That's Burger King, you dope."

"Don't call your sister a dope," warned Mrs. McDonald.

The kids pressed their noses against the window to peer inside. It looked like a real McDonald's, except there were antique milkshake machines, vintage ads, photos about the history of McDonald's on the walls, and some mannequins standing at the counter in old-time uniforms. Pep tried to pull open the door, but it was locked.

"I'm sorry, but the museum is closed today," said a voice behind them.

The McDonald family turned around to see a chunky teenage boy standing before them. He was dressed in the same old-time uniform as the mannequins inside. He had pimples on his face, and a shock of red hair poked out from under his paper hat. The boy looked unmistakably like Archie, the comic-book character. If Archie could be cloned and stuffed, this kid would be the result. He appeared to be a few years older than the twins, maybe sixteen.

"Closed?" said Mrs. McDonald, putting her hands on her hips to indicate annoyance. "We drove all the way from California to see this!"

That wasn't exactly true, but it gave more weight to Mrs. McDonald's indignation.

"Well, you're in luck," said the teenager who looked just like Archie. "Our special mobile french fry exhibit is visiting here today. Your kids will love it!"

He pointed to an eighteen-wheeler truck at the far end of the parking lot. It had a big picture of Ronald McDonald on the side, and the words THE MULTIMEDIA WORLD OF FRENCH FRIES.

That seemed to mollify Mrs. McDonald somewhat. She took her hands off her hips.

"Maybe we should go eat first before we do this," Dr. McDonald said. "We're all pretty hungry for dinner."

"This exhibit will only be here for a little while," the teenager said. "I have to go set up another exhibit in Washington. And I'm sorry, but the demonstration is just for kids thirteen and under. No grown-ups allowed."

"Today is our birthday!" Pep said. "We just turned thirteen."

"Well, happy birthday!" the Archie clone said. "The french fry show takes only about half an hour. Do you want to see it?"

"How much does it cost?" Mrs. McDonald asked as she fished in her purse for her wallet.

"It's completely free," the kid said as he pulled two tickets out of his pocket. "Come on, you deserve a break today."

"Of *course* it's free," Dr. McDonald grumbled. "It's a half-hour commercial for McDonald's. They use it to get innocent children addicted to fast food. They should pay *us* to let our kids see this junk."

"I don't know if I want to do it," Pep said, eyeing the eighteen-wheeler.

"Oh, go ahead, honey," encouraged Mrs. McDonald. "It sounds like fun. While you're in there, your dad and I can go check out the Square Deal Shoe Store. I read in the guidebook that the tallest man in the world, Robert Wadlow, used to live around here. He wore size twenty-six shoes, and they have one on display at the store. It's just two blocks from here."

While their parents went to look for the largest shoe in the world, Coke and Pep followed Archie clone to the big truck.

"Are you sure we should be doing this?" Pep

whispered to her brother as they walked across the parking lot. "We don't know this kid. He could do anything to us."

"Will you relax for once in your life?" Coke whispered back. "The kid is a nerd. He's harmless. Look at him. He looks just like Archie from the comics."

"You probably think I'm kind of nerdy," Archie clone said.

"No! Not at all!" Coke and Pep said together.

"Guys at school used to make fun of me," he continued, "but it doesn't bother me anymore."

Actually, Coke felt a little sorry for Archie clone, having to wear a silly uniform and drive around doing demonstrations for McDonald's. It seemed like a lousy summer job. And having to walk around your whole life as the spitting image of Archie must be no picnic either.

"It's minimum wage, but there are fringe benefits," Archie clone said, almost as if he could hear what Coke had been thinking.

"I hope we get free samples," Pep whispered to her brother. "Remember the time we went to Hershey Park and they gave us free samples at Chocolate World?"

"That was cool."

"Your Cheeseheads rock," Archie clone said cheerfully. "I'm into hats myself. I've always been fascinated by the things that people choose to wear on their heads. At home I have a collection of hundreds of hats. Do you think that's weird?"

"No," Coke and Pep lied.

"I guess you and your parents drove down through Wisconsin."

"Yeah," Pep said. "We tried cheese curds for the first time."

"Yum!" the Archie clone said. "Can I assume you kids like our french fries too?"

"Oh yes," Pep replied. "We love them."

"At McDonald's, we peel, slice, freeze, and cook two million pounds of potatoes every day," Archie clone told them, having obviously memorized his speech. "Americans consume an average of about fifty pounds of fresh potatoes and thirty pounds of frozen fries each year. McDonald's is the largest buyer of potatoes in the United States."

"Dude, you sure know a lot about french fries," Coke said, hiding a sneer.

"It's my job to know," Archie clone replied.

"Anybody ever say that you look like that character Archie from the comics?" Coke asked.

"Every day," Archie clone replied. "People call me Archie Clone."

Archie Clone pushed a button on the back of the

eighteen-wheeler. The doors swung open to reveal a gigantic display. It was like a rolling museum devoted to all things potato. Video monitors lined the walls, depicting the planting, harvesting, storing, cooking, and eating of potatoes. In the center was an enormous wire basket, like the kind that is used to make french fries.

"This is cool!" Coke said, as the platform they were standing on raised them up to the level of the truck. "Is this one of those virtual reality rides?"

"You might say that," Archie Clone said, pushing the button again to close the door behind them. "It's an interactive, hands-on, 3-D experience, sort of like the ones they have at Disneyland."

He led the twins up a set of stairs and helped them climb into the big wire basket.

"Is it going to be scary?" asked Pep.

"A little," Archie admitted as he closed the top of the basket. "But the scary part doesn't last long. The cool thing is, you'll get to see the process of making french fries, from the point of view of the spud itself."

"Isn't this exciting?" Pep said. "We're going to be like potatoes!"

Coke glanced over at Archie Clone and noticed a wicked little smile at the corners of his mouth. It was at that moment Coke realized he and his sister were *not* on a virtual reality ride. This truck *wasn't* part of the McDonald's museum. They *weren't* at a mobile exhibit about french fries.

They had stumbled into a trap!

"Hey!" Coke shouted, grabbing and shaking the wire basket that now surrounded them. "We changed our minds. We don't want to do this."

But it was too late. Under the basket, gallons of oil had begun to pour into a large pool. Steam was coming off the oil, and it was bubbling. Coke and Pep could smell it. It smelled like something cooking.

"W-what's going on?" Pep stammered, grabbing her brother's hand.

Archie Clone looked at them, grinning from ear to ear.

"This is my favorite part of the job," he said. "Remember those fringe benefits I told you about?"

He pushed a button, and the wire basket dropped a few inches. It was attached to a large motor and gear system.

"You don't even *work* for McDonald's!" Coke shouted, pointing at Archie Clone.

"Nope," he replied. "I work for a different employer. I think you may have heard of him—Dr. Herman Warsaw."

Chapter 3
THE EVIL ARCHIE CLONE

Of course, Coke and Pep knew all about Dr. Herman Warsaw. He was the lunatic who had chased them halfway across the United States, lured them to The House on the Rock, and tried to kill them there. Instead, it was Dr. Warsaw who met his end tumbling out of The Infinity Room to the rocks below.

But none of that mattered right now, because the twins were trapped in a ten-foot-tall wire cage that was hanging a few feet over a pool filled with boiling oil.

See? I *told* you Coke and Pep would be lowered into boiling oil. But you didn't believe me. Maybe you'll trust me from now on.

The gears turned slowly, and the cage dropped a few more inches.

"Help! Help!" Pep screamed as she shook the cage violently. "Let us out!"

"Save your breath," Archie Clone said. "This truck is totally soundproof. A heavy metal band could do a concert in here and the people standing outside wouldn't hear a peep."

"Are you going to drive us somewhere and kill us?" Pep asked desperately.

"No, of course not," Archie Clone replied. "I'm going to kill you right here. Or to be more specific, I'm going to *fry* you right here. Hey, you kids aren't French by any chance, are you? That would be ironic!"

The cage dropped a few more inches. Pep shrieked and began to climb up the sides. Coke desperately looked around for a way out. The bottom of the cage was about a foot above the boiling oil.

"Dr. Warsaw is dead!" Coke shouted at Archie Clone. "We were there! We saw it happen! You don't need to kill us anymore!"

"It doesn't matter to me if Dr. Warsaw is dead or alive," Archie Clone said, still smiling.

"Then why are you doing this?" Pep yelled. "We never did anything to you. We never even met you before today."

"True, you didn't," Archie Clone said, "but the three of us have something in common."

"What?" Coke asked.

"TGF," Archie Clone said. "You know what that stands for, don't you?"

The Genius Files.

"You're one of *us*?" Pep shouted. The cage dropped a few more inches, and she climbed higher. The top of the cage prevented her from climbing all the way out.

"That's right," Archie Clone said calmly, "and soon I'll be the *only* one of us."

As part of The Genius Files program (which you would know if you had read *The Genius Files: Mission Unstoppable*), Dr. Warsaw had selected a small group of the brightest children in America. One of these kids might be sitting next to you right now as you read this book. These "gifted and talented" kids were identified using standardized testing in schools all over the country. Coke and Pep were singled out. They hadn't met any of the other kids in the program . . . until now.

The cage dropped a few more inches, so the bottom of it was now below the level of the boiling oil. Pep screamed. Coke followed his sister's lead, climbing up the wire to avoid the bubbling oil.

"So your plan is to kill all the Genius Files kids?" Coke asked.

"That's right."

"Why?" Coke asked. "What could that possibly accomplish?"

"Stop talking with him!" Pep screamed at her brother. "Find a way to get us out of here!"

"Oh hush, Pep," said Archie Clone. "There's no way out. I'm sure they told you when you joined The Genius Files that you would get a million dollars when you turn twenty-one years old, right?"

"Yeah, so?" said Coke.

"What they didn't tell you is that it's not a million dollars for each of us. It's a million dollars for *all* of us. We'll *split* it evenly. So let's say there are a thousand kids who are members of The Genius Files. Do you know what a million dollars divided by a thousand works out to?"

Pep moved the decimal point in her head.

"A thousand dollars," she said.

"That's right," Archie Clone said. "You *are* pretty smart! Now, I don't know about you two, but I'm not going to put my life on the line for a lousy thousand bucks when I turn twenty-one."

"So the more Genius Files kids who die before they reach twenty-one, the more money each survivor gets," Coke reasoned.

"Hey, you're catchin' on, big guy!" said Archie

Clone. "And if I happen to be the only survivor, well, it doesn't take a genius to figure out what happens."

"You get *all* the money!" Pep shouted. "You're evil!"

"He's also insane," Coke added.

"Insane?" Archie Clone said, laughing. "Your mother drove halfway across the country to visit a mustard museum. And *I'm* the crazy one?"

"How did *you* know about that?" Pep demanded.

"Oh, I know all about you two," Archie Clone said, smiling. "I do my homework, like a good boy."

"How many other Genius Files kids are still alive?" Coke asked. "How many have you killed?"

"That's none of your concern," Archie Clone said.

The cage lowered a few more inches and Pep screamed again. The twins pressed themselves tightly against the top.

"*Do* something, Coke!" Pep shouted.

"What do you want me to do?" he yelled back at her. "Why don't *you* figure something out for a change?"

"I didn't want to come inside this stupid truck in the first place!" she said angrily. "I knew this was going to be trouble. You told me to relax and have fun!"

"I did not!"

"I wish you two would stop bickering," Archie Clone said. "It's giving me a headache. Just think of this as a ride. Like at a theme park. Except that at the end, you don't get ice cream or cotton candy. You *die*. Ha, ha!"

He cackled an evil laugh as if he had heard it in the movies.

"Let us out!" Pep begged as the boiling oil rose inside the cage.

"Oh, what are you complaining about?" Archie Clone said. "The admission was free. Ha, ha! So put a smile on."

"You're sick, dude," Coke said. "You know that? Genius and insanity go hand in hand. You should get help."

"Oh, thanks for your expert analysis, Dr. Freud," Archie Clone said sarcastically. "I don't know what you're so upset about, Coke. You were going to die anyway. Now you'll just get it over with, seventy years early. No point in waiting until the last minute, right? Ha, ha!"

"My sneakers are heating up!" Pep yelled. "I can feel it."

The greasy oil was smoking and spitting as it rose, splattering the twins.

"Don't worry," Archie Clone called out, "I don't use any trans fats. You'll be dead soon, but at least you'll die with low cholesterol. Ha, ha!"

"You'll never get away with this!" Coke told him.

"The police will be here any second."

"You're right about that," Archie Clone said. "I must be going. It wouldn't look good if I was here when the police find your deep-fried bodies."

"I hate you!" Pep shouted.

Archie Clone ignored her and pushed a button on a remote control, which caused a trap door to open in the floor about ten feet behind him.

"Have a nice life . . . what's left of it!" he said as he lowered himself through the hole. "Ha, ha! I'm lovin' it!"

Archie Clone jumped down through the hole, and the trap door shut over him. This was *bad*. The one person who could save them, who happened to also be the one person who was trying to kill them, was gone. The cage continued to lower itself into the oil. Now it was inches from their bottoms as they clung to the top of the cage. Sweat was pouring off them, dripping into the boiling oil, and splattering them.

"What are we gonna do?" Pep yelled to her brother. "Do you have anything? A tool? A Frisbee? Anything?"

"Yeah, I happen to have a chain saw in my pocket," Coke replied sarcastically.

"Oh, great!"

"What would we do with a Frisbee anyway?" Coke

asked sharply. "Have a catch to help us forget that we're about to become human french fries?"

"I don't know," Pep said. "Maybe you could jam the Frisbee into those gears or something. Stop the machine."

Coke looked at the gear mechanism outside the cage. It was about two feet away, turning slowly. He could reach it, but that wouldn't do any good, unless he was willing to give up a few fingers for the cause.

But then he got an idea.

"Give me your Cheesehead!" he barked.

"What for?"

"Just give it to me!"

Coke grabbed the foam Cheesehead off Pep's head and carefully climbed over his sister to the part of the cage that was closest to the gear mechanism. The Cheesehead was a little bit too big to fit through the openings in the cage, but it was spongy enough so Coke could squeeze it between the bars.

"Be careful!" Pep said.

"Hold on tight," Coke ordered her.

He reached his right arm outside the cage and extended the Cheesehead toward the turning gears. Then he pushed the corner of the Cheesehead right between two gears.

The gears bit into the Cheesehead, ripping at the

yellow foam. For a moment, it looked like the gears would simply chew the Cheesehead to tiny pieces without slowing down the mechanism. But then there was a groaning noise, a lurch, and the gears stopped turning. They had literally bitten off more than they could chew.

"It stopped!" Pep shouted gleefully. "We're saved!"

"Not yet," Coke said.

He still had to climb over to the other side of the cage and open a latch that was holding the top on. After struggling for a few minutes and nearly falling into the boiling oil below him, Coke managed to force open the latch and push up the top of the cage. He climbed out and then extended a hand down to pull his sister up after him. They jumped off the top and landed on the floor without getting hurt. The cage was almost completely submerged in oil.

"Let's get out of here," Coke said.

Moments after they pushed open a door and ran out of the truck, Coke and Pep spotted their parents in the parking lot, walking excitedly back to the RV.

"Oh, you kids missed something great," Dr. McDonald told them.

"You should have seen it!" said Mrs. McDonald. "We found the shoe store. This guy Robert Wadlow was eight feet, eleven inches tall. His foot was *enormous*. It was three feet long. Imagine that! A foot was three feet. Just amazing."

"How was the virtual french fry demonstration?" asked Dr. McDonald.

"Very . . . exciting," Coke said honestly.

"Yeah, we really got to feel what it must be like to be a french fry," said Pep.

"Where's your Cheesehead?" Mrs. McDonald asked her.

"I . . . uh . . . lost it," she replied. It was true, technically.

"I paid $14.99 for that Cheesehead!" Dr. McDonald complained, his voice rising.

"Don't be mad, Ben," his wife said. "It's their birthday."

"You're right," he said with a sigh.

It's hard to be mad at somebody on their birthday. All Pep did was lose her silly Cheesehead. It wasn't like she murdered anybody or anything.

"Hey, how about we go to McDonald's for dinner?" asked Mrs. McDonald. "I bet you're really in the mood for french fries after seeing that demonstration, huh?"

The twins looked at each other.

"We're not hungry," they said simultaneously.

Chapter 4
THE
FIRST
CIPHER

It had been a long day. A *ridiculously* long day. It seemed like ages ago when Coke and Pep were being chased through The House on the Rock by Mrs. Higgins, their evil health teacher. They had clotheslined her with a piece of twine stretched across a walkway in the dark. Then they were grabbed by those two bowler dude maniacs dressed in suits of armor, who dragged them to Dr. Warsaw. He would have killed them for sure if they hadn't snatched away his portable electronic torture device and pushed him out of the hole in the bottom of The

Infinity Room. And now, this Archie Clone lunatic had nearly deep-fried them in a pool filled with boiling oil.

Some birthday.

The next scheduled stop was Chicago, just twenty miles away. But it's hard to find a place to park an RV overnight in such a big city. So Dr. McDonald decided to splurge and have the family spend the night at a motel in Des Plaines. He pulled into Best Western Des Plaines Inn, just down the road on Lee Street. It would be nice to sleep in a regular bed for a change. Instead of jamming the whole family into one room, they got two—one for the kids and one for the grown-ups.

Go to Google Maps (http://maps.google.com/).

Click Get Directions.

In the A box, type Des Plaines IL.

In the B box, type Chicago IL.

Click Get Directions.

The twins didn't ask for cake or ice cream or some sweet treat to top off their birthday. All they wanted to do was go to sleep, and try to forget what had happened over the last twenty-four hours. They were exhausted.

Before Coke took off his pants, he checked the

pockets and found the tickets that Archie Clone had given him for the french fry exhibit. He turned one of them over and saw this written on the back:

HATED DAY HAPPY

Coke puzzled over the three words for a minute, and then handed the ticket to his sister.

"What do you think this means?" he asked.

Pep looked the tickets over. "It doesn't make any sense," she said.

"Do you think it's just random words?"

"It may be meaningless," Pep replied, "or it may be a cipher."

"Oh no. Not *another* one," Coke groaned.

Pep *loved* ciphers. While Coke's brain excelled at accumulating and storing huge quantities of information, Pep was good at organizing and analyzing it. She loved word games, number games, and trying to untangle secret messages and codes. She was fascinated by anything to do with spies and spying.

During their drive from California, every few days Dr. Warsaw had sent them a coded message, which Pep was always able to decipher. That's how they knew to go to The Infinity Room at The House on the Rock. Some of the messages were harder to decipher than others.

But Dr. Warsaw was dead. Or at least they *assumed*

he was dead. Maybe he wasn't. Maybe he was alive and HATED DAY HAPPY was another secret message from him. Or maybe he had created the message before he died. Or maybe somebody *else* had taken over the Genius Files operation and was sending them ciphers now. Who knew?

Pep pulled out her notebook, lay down on the bed, and wrote out the letters. She stared at them. The cipher seemed pretty straightforward. It didn't look like a particularly difficult code to crack.

She turned the letters backward—YPPAH YAD DETAH. Nope, that was meaningless. She wrote down every other letter, and then every third letter. She held a mirror up to the words. She transposed the letters, and then tried jumbling them around randomly. Nothing worked. Everything she did to the cipher made it look less like real words than it had at the start. She was feeling sleepy, like her brain was working at half speed.

And then, just before her eyes were about to close for the night, she figured it out.

"I got it," she whispered to Coke. "It's a simple anagram."

Then she wrote something in her notebook and handed it to her brother.

HAPPY DEATH DAY

Chapter 5

UNEXPECTED GUESTS

It wasn't until the next morning, when the twins woke up in their motel room, that they were able to fully comprehend the seriousness of their situation. Getting rid of Dr. Warsaw at The House on the Rock had not solved their problem, as they had thought. No, their problem had just begun. People were *still* after them. Coke and Pep would have to live with that fact, maybe until they themselves were dead, or the people who were trying to kill them were dead. Maybe it was just Archie Clone who was after them now. Or maybe Mrs. Higgins and the bowler dudes were still out there somewhere too. Maybe there were others as well.

It makes it kind of hard to get through your everyday life, knowing that at any moment somebody might try to throw you off a cliff, dip you into boiling oil, drown you in a vat of SPAM, or bury you alive in a sand dune. That's no way to live.

"We gotta tell Mom and Dad," Coke said to his sister as they brushed their teeth that morning. "This isn't some game. The game is over. Mom and Dad will know what to do."

"Agreed."

After showering and getting dressed, Coke and Pep knocked on the door of their parents' room. Dr. and Mrs. McDonald were already dressed and ready to go downstairs to the little breakfast room next to the motel lobby. They were in the middle of a discussion about Dr. McDonald's next book. His last one, *The Impact of Coal on the Industrial Revolution*, had not sold very well.

"Honey, maybe you should write about something a little more . . . commercial next time," Mrs. McDonald suggested delicately.

"What, like Britney Spears?" Dr. McDonald replied with sarcasm in his voice. "Maybe I should write a book about Lindsay Lohan's love life. Lots of people would buy that."

"No, Ben, I mean—"

"We need to talk to you about something," Coke told his parents.

"What is it, sweetie?" Mrs. McDonald said with concern as they made their way to the breakfast room.

Coke took a deep breath.

"You may find this a little hard to believe," he began, "but Pep and I are part of a secret government program. It's called The Genius Files."

Silence. They continued up to the buffet line to get their food.

"Go on," urged Dr. McDonald.

"Ever since we left California," Pep told them, "there have been these crazy people who have been trying to kill us. They forced us to jump off a cliff back home . . ."

". . . and they blew up a building we were in right next to our favorite Chinese restaurant . . . ," Coke said.

". . . and they left us to die at the singing sand dune . . . ," Pep added.

". . . and they tried to drown us at the SPAM Museum . . ."

". . . and they tried to boil us in oil yesterday—"

Dr. McDonald held up his hand to stop them.

"So, you're telling us that these people are still out there," he said, "and that your lives are in danger."

"Right," Pep said. "We would have told you about

all this earlier, but we had been sworn to secrecy."

They sat down at a table.

"We have GPS devices implanted in our heads," Coke added, "so the bad guys who are trying to kill us know where we are at all times."

Dr. and Mrs. McDonald stared at the twins for a long time.

Then they burst out in hysterical laughter.

"Hooo! Hooo!" Dr. McDonald said through the tears that were streaming down his face. "That's a good one! GPS devices in your heads!"

"It's not even April Fools' Day!" said Mrs. McDonald as she wiped her face with a napkin. "How do you kids come up with this stuff? You two are so imaginative!"

"No, we mean it!" Coke protested. "We're totally serious!"

"You guys crack me up," Dr. McDonald said, unable to stop laughing. "Bridge, I'm so glad we changed our minds and decided to have children after all. Our kids never cease to amaze me."

"They do say the darndest things," said Mrs. McDonald.

So much for that idea. It didn't look like their parents were going to be any help at all. Coke and Pep would have to live . . . or die . . . on their own.

As their parents chuckled and lingered over their coffee, the twins went outside to talk things over privately.

"What are we gonna do now?" Pep asked.

"How should I know?"

"Maybe we should call the police."

"Are you out of your mind? They'll *never* believe us," Coke told her. "Mom and Dad didn't even believe us. You think the cops will?"

Ever since they were little, Coke had been the "big brother," even though he was only a few minutes older. Pep had come to rely on him to get them out of jams using his mouth, his fists, a deck of cards, a Cheesehead, or whatever happened to be lying around.

Now, though, Coke worried about what was going to happen next. That Archie Clone who'd tried to french fry them could be anywhere. He could be watching them right now, or listening in on their conversations. They would have to track him down. They might have to kill him, before he killed them.

And what about Mrs. Higgins? What about those crazy bowler dudes? What about the other Genius Files kids who might be gunning for them so they could claim the million dollars?

And what about Dr. Warsaw? Maybe he had

survived the fall and was out there somewhere, concocting more intricate secret messages and plans to kill them.

As the twins walked back to their room to pack up their stuff and check out of the motel, two maids were blocking the hallway with big carts loaded up with towels, cleaning supplies, and those little plastic shampoo bottles they leave in the rooms.

"Excuse me," Pep said politely, assuming that would be enough to send the message that they needed to get past.

The maids didn't turn around. One was holding a broom and the other was fiddling with a vacuum cleaner.

"Pardon me," Coke said, a little more forcefully. "We need to get to our room."

"No speakee Engleesh," said one of the maids in a vague accent.

Coke rolled his eyes and pushed his way past the two carts, and gestured for Pep to follow him. That's when both maids clapped their hands over the twins' mouths and grabbed them forcefully from behind.

"What the—"

"Keep your mouth shut and you won't get hurt!" one of the "maids" grunted in a male voice as Pep tried to bite the hand over her mouth.

"Let us go!" Pep tried to holler.

The maids dragged Coke and Pep roughly down the hall and used a key to open a door with no room number on it. Then they shoved the twins into the room, followed them inside, and slammed the door behind them. It was a storage room, with racks filled with towels on the walls.

"Who are you?" Pep demanded. "What do you want from us?"

The maids ripped wigs off their heads and smiled broadly.

"Mya!" yelled Pep.

"Bones!" yelled Coke.

Now, if you had read *The Genius Files: Mission Unstoppable*, you would know who Bones and Mya are. If you didn't read that book, well, maybe next time you'll listen when I tell you to do something.

Bones was the custodian at the twins' school who had watched over them and initiated them into The Genius Files program. Mya was also on The Genius Files team. It was Mya who had given them wingsuits so they would survive their plunge over the cliff back home in California.

There were hugs all around. The twins were grateful to see them, even if Bones did look a little strange wearing a maid's uniform.

"Do you work here at the motel?" Pep asked.

"Of *course* they don't work here, you dope!" Coke said. "They're disguised as maids so people won't know who they really are."

"We're undercover," Bones said. "I'm glad to see you two are alive and well."

"Barely," Pep said. "Yesterday this crazy teenager trapped us in a giant french fry cage and tried to drop us into boiling oil. What a way to celebrate our birthday."

"Happy birthday!" Mya said cheerfully. "We wanted to get you presents, but we didn't have time."

"Saving our lives would have been a nice present," Coke said as he pulled the ticket to the french fry simulator out of his pocket and showed it to Bones and Mya.

"'Hated day happy,'" Bones read off the ticket. "What do you think that means?"

"I figured it out," Pep said. "It means 'happy death day.'"

"This teenager who tried to kill you," Mya said. "What did he look like?"

"He was kind of nerdy-looking, chubby, and he had bright red hair," Pep told them. "Like Archie, from the comics."

Bones and Mya looked at each other.

"Archie Clone," they said together.

"You know that kid?" Coke said.

"Oh yeah," Bones said. "We know him. The Genius Files kid. The renegade."

"This is precisely the reason why Dr. Warsaw had to end The Genius Files program," Mya told them. "He thought he would simply recruit genius kids from all over the country to solve America's problems, and they would do whatever he told them. But kids don't always do what we grown-ups tell them to do. And geniuses like Archie Clone, well, you never know what crazy thing they might do."

"We suspect that he might be criminally insane," Bones added.

"Kids made fun of him at school," Coke said. "Maybe that's what messed him up."

"How did Archie Clone get that big truck?" Pep asked. "And all that french fry apparatus? It must have cost somebody a fortune."

"He figured out a way," Bones said. "He's a very bright and resourceful young man. Some say he's trying to follow in Dr. Warsaw's footsteps. He may be trying to take over The Genius Files program now that Dr. Warsaw is gone."

"He told us he was going to kill off all The Genius Files kids," Pep said, "so that when he turns twenty-one, he'll be the only one left and he'll get to keep the million dollars."

Bones whistled.

"Did he say anything else?"

Coke and Pep thought back, trying to remember anything Archie Clone had said that might be important. Pep couldn't think of anything, but suddenly Coke snapped his fingers.

"He did say two things."

"What?"

"One, he collects hats," Coke said, "and two, he said he had to give us the tour right away because he was on his way to Washington."

"Washington, D.C., or Washington State?" Mya asked.

"He didn't say," Coke replied.

"Probably D.C.," Bones said.

"That's where we're heading," Pep said.

"So are we," said Mya. "We've got to stop him before he hurts anybody."

"How are we going to do that?" asked Coke.

"We don't know," Bones replied.

"How are we going to find him?" asked Pep.

"We don't know that either," replied Mya.

"You don't know a whole lot, do you?" said Coke.

"We'll be in touch," Bones said. "You kids can relax now. Try to enjoy your vacation. Have fun with your parents. Mya and I will head for Washington. Hopefully this whole thing will be over before you get there."

"Can you give us a cell phone number or some way to reach you?" asked Pep.

"Too dangerous," Mya replied. "We are constantly being monitored."

"Here," Bones said as he reached into the maid's cart and handed the twins a plastic bag, "take some of these."

"You're giving us little bars of soap?" Pep asked as she looked into the bag.

"It's not plain old soap, you dope!" Coke told her. "It's *exploding* soap, right? You throw it at somebody and it can take their head off. Like a hand grenade. That stuff is *cool*."

"It's not exploding soap," Bones told him.

"I know," Coke said. "It's special GPS soap. You plant it on somebody and then you can track them, even when they're in the shower. And then it melts away without leaving a trace. How do you people come up with this stuff? It's brilliant!"

"Uh, no," said Mya, "there's no such thing as GPS soap."

"I know," Coke said excitedly. "You put two of them over your eyes and they function as night-vision goggles, right?"

"It's just *soap*," Bones said wearily.

"What are we supposed to do with plain old *soap*?" Coke demanded.

"You *wash* yourselves with it," Bones said. "I figured it might come in handy in your RV."

"How do you expect us to save the world with little bars of soap?" Coke asked. "We need some weapons, and preferably *cool* weapons, like the kind they have in action movies."

"We don't have any cool weapons," Mya said. "This is strictly a low-budget operation."

"Hey, you're the ones who are geniuses," Bones told them. "You figure it out. We need to go now."

"Before we leave I need to ask you something," Mya said. "Did you tell your parents anything about The Genius Files?"

"We tried to, but they didn't believe us," Pep replied.

"Good," Mya said. "They must not know. Ever. If they find out, their lives will be in danger too."

"Hey, one last thing we need to know before you go," Coke said. "Is Dr. Warsaw dead or alive?"

"We think he's dead, but we're not sure," Bones said. "We searched for his body in the woods around The House on the Rock, but by the time we got there, it was gone."

"Good luck," Mya said, hugging each of the twins.

"Be careful. We are with you always."

"If you're with us," Coke said, "you would give us some of those Frisbee grenades you have, or a flame-thrower, or something that we could actually use to defend ourselves."

"Goodness no," said Mya. "That would be danger-ous!"

"Then at least clean our room," Pep said. "It's a mess."

Chapter 6
LET'S
KILL
TWO

Mrs. McDonald checked out of the motel while her husband loaded up the RV and consulted his road atlas. Everybody piled in and Dr. McDonald pulled onto I-294 South. Des Plaines is only about half an hour from downtown Chicago.

The kids amused themselves in the back while Mrs. McDonald fired up the GPS. Then she reclined her seat a few inches and began to leaf through an Illinois guidebook.

"Look, Ben," Mrs. McDonald said, "the grave of Robert Earl Hughes is in Illinois."

"Who was he?" Pep asked, not quite sure she wanted to know the answer.

"Robert Earl Hughes was the world's heaviest man," her mother explained. "He weighed over a thousand pounds. Poor guy. He was only thirty-two when he died. They say he was buried in a grand piano."

Unfortunately, the grave site of this amazing man was in Benville, over four hours away. It was tempting to go there, but in life you have to set your priorities. Four hours would be a long drive to see a gravestone, even if it was the gravestone of somebody who was buried in a piano.

Equally tempting, at least for Mrs. McDonald, would have been a trip to see the world's largest statue of Abraham Lincoln, in Ashmore, Illinois. And then, of course, there was the Grain Elevator Museum in Atlanta, Illinois. But that was 154 miles away, and in the wrong direction. Nobody had the enthusiasm to drive so far.

154

"It's a shame we're going to miss those grain elevators, Mom," Coke said, sharing a silent giggle with his sister. "They sound really cool."

None of the McDonalds was conscious of it, but there was one thing they all wanted to see—a city. Ever since they'd left California a week earlier, they had been driving past deserts, prairies, billboards, cornfields, dairy farms, and lots of small towns. They missed the excitement of a city.

Soon, the suburbs gave way to office parks, the office parks gave way to the enormous O'Hare Airport, and from Route 90 East the majestic skyline of Chicago came into view.

"The Windy City!" Coke proclaimed.

"The City of the Big Shoulders," said Dr. McDonald. "That's how Carl Sandburg described it."

"Didn't he play for the Cubs?" asked Coke.

"That was Ryne Sandberg," Dr. McDonald corrected him. "Carl Sandburg was a poet."

"Ha!" Pep proclaimed to her brother. "You don't know everything!"

"Okay, here's today's agenda," Mrs. McDonald announced from the front seat. "First, the International Museum of Surgical Science. They have antique instruments that doctors used to drill holes in skulls, and they also have some skulls with holes drilled into them. And get this—they've got a copy of the death mask of Napoleon! It will be perfect for *Amazing but True*."

"That place sounds gross, Mom," Pep commented, despite her fascination with morbid things. It was Pep, after all, who'd convinced the family to visit the

Donner Party exhibit back in Nevada—which was all about cannibals.

"Second, the Museum of Science and Industry," Mrs. McDonald continued. "They have an exhibit called Body Slices. It says here they have male and female cadavers, each cut into half-inch slices and preserved between sheets of glass."

"Ugh!" said Pep, despite her obvious fascination. "That is disgusting, Mom. We don't want to look at that stuff!"

"Well, the good news is, you don't have to," Mrs. McDonald said cheerfully. "*I'm* going to look at that stuff."

"Where are the rest of us going?" asked Pep.

Dr. McDonald leaned over, pulled three tickets out of the glove compartment, and waved them in the air.

"Wrigley Field, baby!" he yelled.

"We're going to see the Cubs play?" asked Coke excitedly. "All right!"

Dr. McDonald dropped his wife off at the Loop in downtown Chicago and proceeded up North Lake Shore Drive until he found a parking lot that would admit recreational vehicles and wasn't too far from the ballpark. They got out and walked the rest of the way to the corner of North Clark Street and West Addison.

"This is historic ground," Dr. McDonald said, throwing an arm around each of his children. "It's one of the oldest Major League ballparks still standing. Babe Ruth hit his famous 'called shot' home run here back in 1932, you know."

"Can we get cotton candy?" asked Pep, no big fan of baseball.

"Sure," her dad replied. "As far as I'm concerned, it's still your birthday today."

The game had already started, so they rushed inside to find their seats on the third-base side. Dr. McDonald bought cotton candy for both twins and pointed out the distinctive ivy-covered outfield walls.

Wrigley Field felt like a sanctuary to Coke and Pep.

Here, for a change, they could forget their troubles—lunatics in bowler hats, evil health teachers, maniacal teenagers who resembled comic-book characters—for a few hours at least.

The ballpark was packed. The visiting team was the St. Louis Cardinals, longtime rivals of the Cubs. The crowd went wild when the Cubs scored a couple of runs in the second inning. When the Cards tied it up in the third, boos rained down on the field.

When that inning was over, Dr. McDonald told the kids to look at the video screen below the scoreboard. This message was flashing:

HAPPY 13TH BIRTHDAY YESTERDAY TO COKE AND PEP McDONALD!

Then, next to those words, the "Fan Cam" box appeared and there was a video image of Coke and Pep. When they saw themselves on the screen, they smiled and waved. Everybody cheered.

"How did they know it was our birthday?" Pep said excitedly.

"I called ahead," Dr. McDonald said.

"Isn't that expensive, Dad?" Coke asked.

"Don't worry about it," Dr. McDonald replied. "One of my old college buddies works for the Cubs."

The message flashed several more times, and then the screen faded to black. A few seconds later, it was replaced by this message:

⊐⊃◡⌐∟∧⊃⊓<⊰ ⊐⊓⌐☐⊐

Everyone stared at the video screen, confused.

"Huh?" said Dr. McDonald. "I wonder what *that* means."

"Hey, check it out!" somebody a few rows behind them hollered. "The guy running the video screen musta had too many beers!"

Coke squinted at the message and looked over at his sister quizzically.

"It looks like a cipher," Pep whispered in his ear so their father would not hear.

"What does it mean?" Coke whispered back.

"How should I know?"

"Well, you're the queen of the ciphers," Coke whispered. "You're supposed to be good at this stuff."

"This stuff takes time," Pep told him.

The message disappeared from the screen and was replaced by an ad for a Chicago pizza parlor. Luckily, Coke had gazed at it long enough to burn the symbols into his memory.

"Somebody knows we're here," Pep whispered nervously to her brother. "We need to go."

"Dad, can we leave?" Coke asked.

"Leave?" he replied. "It's only the top of the fourth inning! Let's at least stay until the seventh inning stretch."

"Okay," the twins grumbled.

For the next two innings, Coke and Pep had little interest in watching the ball game. They were too busy scanning the crowd, looking out for guys with bowler hats, evil health teachers, Archie Clones, or perhaps even Dr. Herman Warsaw. Their names and faces had been up on the video screen. There was no telling who might be watching them through binoculars from some distant point in the ballpark—or what that person might be planning. They were strangely quiet while eating hot dogs their father bought from a vendor.

The Cardinals scored three runs in the fifth, and the mood of the crowd was turning sour. There's nothing more dangerous than an angry Cubs fan. You would think that after a hundred years without winning a World Series, they would get used to losing ball games. But they never do.

It was 6–2 at the end of the sixth inning, when a female usher came over to their row and tapped Coke and Pep on their shoulders. They both jumped.

"Would you two come with me, please?" the usher

said sweetly. "We have something special for you."

Pep looked at her father, terrified. Surely he would protect them.

"Go ahead," Dr. McDonald said, a big smile on his face. "This is part of your birthday present too. Have fun."

The twins got up and followed the usher up the steps and through a doorway. There was a tunnel there that led to the press boxes.

"What's this all about?" Coke asked.

"Nobody told you?" said the usher. "You're in for a treat. Your dad must know somebody pretty important. They don't let just *anybody* lead the crowd in 'Take Me Out to the Ball Game' during the seventh inning stretch!"

"Ohhhhhhhhhhhhh!" the twins said.

The usher led them to a private booth on the press level and opened the door with a key.

"Sing loud!" she said before leaving.

A woman was sitting in the booth, looking out at the field. There was a microphone on the shelf in front of her, and a bottle of Purell. When the door opened, she swiveled around in her chair.

"Mrs. Higgins!" Pep screamed, shrinking back in horror.

Coke quickly grabbed for the doorknob, but it

wouldn't turn. They were locked in the little booth, and their evil health teacher was sitting no more than three feet away from them! They had no weapons, and not even a Frisbee or a deck of cards to defend themselves.

Mrs. Higgins was wearing a Cubs shirt and had a big smile on her face.

"Well, if it isn't Coke and Pep, the McDonald twins," she said pleasantly. "Fancy meeting *you* here!"

There was a four-inch horizontal scar that went across the front of her neck, and she touched it involuntarily.

"You leave us alone!" Coke said, getting into a defensive stance and pointing his finger at her. He was ready for anything. "You remember what happened the last time you messed with us!"

"Calm down, Coke!" Mrs. Higgins said, laughing. "I've retired from the paid assassin business."

"Retired?" Pep asked. "Are you putting us on?"

"I got sick of it," Mrs. Higgins said. "All of it. Chasing kids all over the country. Setting schools on fire. Luring unsuspecting victims into diabolical traps. It's *exhausting*. And do you think Dr. Warsaw ever paid me a dime in overtime, or paid for my health insurance? Forget about it! I was glad you two got rid of him. It gave me the motivation I needed to start a new career. To try something different."

"Do you mean it?" Pep asked, not quite sure if Mrs. Higgins could be trusted.

"Sure," Mrs. Higgins said. "That's why I applied for this job working in the public relations department. It gives me the chance to use my people skills."

"People skills?" Coke said. "You tried to kill us!"

As Mrs. Higgins laughed heartily, the twins noticed the name tag on her shirt: AUDREY HIGGINS, PUBLIC RELATIONS DEPT., CHICAGO CUBS.

"You and I may have had our petty disagreements," she said, "but it's all water under the bridge. That's my philosophy. I'm willing to let bygones be bygones. Any problems we had with each other in the past are history, as far as I'm concerned."

"It was just *yesterday*!" Coke said.

"Come on," Mrs. Higgins said, reaching into a drawer in front of her, "lighten up. We have these free Cubs T-shirts for the people who sing 'Take Me Out to the Ball Game.'"

She handed Coke and Pep the shirts. They looked at each other for a moment, to see what the other one was going to do.

"Go ahead. Put 'em on," said Mrs. Higgins. "It's almost time to sing."

As the twins put the T-shirts over their shirts, the

Cardinals made the third out in the top of the seventh inning.

That's when Mrs. Higgins suddenly pulled out a gun and pointed it at Coke and Pep.

The smile was gone from her face. She looked like a different person.

"Now it's time for you to *die!*"

"What?!" Coke exclaimed, sticking his hands in the air.

"You little punks killed my fiancé!" she barked.

"You and Dr. Warsaw were going to be . . . *married*?" Pep sputtered. "We didn't know—"

"He was the only man I ever loved!" Mrs. Higgins said, her eyes watery. "And you killed him!"

"It was self-defense!" Coke explained. "He was trying to kill us!"

"I've got news for you little twerps," Mrs. Higgins said, leaning in close and sticking the gun in Coke's face. "I put a bomb under the bench in the Cubs dugout. It's programmed to go off when you sing the phrase 'One, two, three strikes you're out.'"

"What?! Are you crazy?"

"Please rise," the public address announcer said. "Today, Coke and Pep McDonald of Point Reyes Station, California, will lead us in the traditional singing of 'Take Me Out to the Ball Game.'"

An organ played the familiar introduction to the song. Coke and Pep looked at each other. Mrs. Higgins pushed the microphone closer to them with one hand and the gun closer to them with the other.

"Sing!" she ordered.

"*Take me out to the ball game*," the twins croaked out the first line.

The crowd began to boo. Pep had her eyes closed in terror. She could barely speak, much less sing another line.

"I said *sing!*" Mrs. Higgins ordered.

"*Take me out to the crowd . . .*"

"Keep singing or I'll blow your heads off!" Mrs. Higgins sneered, brandishing the pistol.

"*Buy me some peanuts and Cracker Jack . . .*"

"Those kids stink!" somebody shouted.

"Sing!" Mrs. Higgins ordered. Tears were rolling down Pep's cheeks.

"*I don't care if I never get back . . .*"

"Those kids sing worse than Ozzy Osbourne!" somebody yelled.

"Sing!" Mrs. Higgins said, sticking the gun into Coke's ribs.

"*Root, root, root for the home team. If they don't win it's a shame . . .*"

"Now *finish* it!" Mrs. Higgins ordered. "It's the Cubs . . . or *you*!"

"For it's one . . . two . . ."

At that point, Coke grabbed the microphone.

"There's a bomb in the Cubs dugout!" he shouted quickly. "Under the bench! Get out! Evacuate the dugout! Evacuate the stadium! This is not a joke! There's a bomb!"

Down on the field, the Cub players came running out of their dugout. In the stands, people got out of their seats and rushed for the exits.

Quickly, it became bedlam at Wrigley Field. Hot dog vendors were getting knocked over. Little kids and old ladies were getting trampled.

In the booth, Mrs. Higgins threw back her head and laughed. Then she took a bite out of her gun.

"It was fake?" Coke yelled. "You mean to tell me there's no bomb in the dugout?"

"Mmm, I am such a chocoholic," said Mrs. Higgins

as she took another bite out of the gun.

Down on the field, a bomb squad in full protective gear was tearing apart the Cubs dugout, throwing bats, gloves, and seat cushions every which way.

The game had been officially called on account of a bomb scare. The Cardinals had won. The Cub fans, who were already angry, were now furious as they streamed out the exits.

"Why did you do that?" Pep asked.

Mrs. Higgins glared at her with a look that sent shivers down Pep's spine.

"Herman Warsaw was the kindest, gentlest, most loving man I ever met," she spat. "We were going to spend the rest of our lives together. So now I'm going to make the rest of your lives a living hell, until the day that you die. And you can count on that being *very* soon. Let's see if you can make it out of this ball-park in one piece."

She opened the door with a key, and the twins ran out of the booth. They located the first exit sign and headed down the ramp, along with hundreds of Chicago's beloved bleacher bums.

"Hey!" somebody shouted. "It's *them*! The kids who made the bomb scare!"

"We forfeited the game because of them!"

"Let's *get* those kids!"

"Yeah!"

Pep turned around.

"What do we do now?" she asked her brother.

"We get out of here," Coke replied.

The twins dashed down the ramp, passing throngs of disgruntled fans heading for the parking lot.

"Kill them!" somebody shouted. "Kill those kids!"

"These people are angry way out of proportion to what happened," Pep said as Coke grabbed her hand and started running full speed. "It's just a game."

"Not to them!"

Hundreds of people were chasing them out Gate K, some of them waving foam fingers and miniature wooden baseball bats.

"Run!" Coke yelled, sprinting down West Waveland Avenue. "These people are crazy!"

"We have to find Dad!" Pep yelled back.

Coke's cell phone rang. It was his father calling. He didn't pick it up.

"Later!" Coke told his sister. "Let's get out of this neighborhood first."

The twins ran for their lives two blocks down Waveland, then made a right on North Clark Street and a left on West Grace Street. By that time, the angry mob that had been chasing them had fallen back. The twins ducked into an alley and stopped, panting and gasping for breath. It was only then that they noticed what it said on the back of the T-shirts Mrs. Higgins had given them.

THE CUBS SUCK!

Chapter 7
"DON'T STOP 'TIL YOU GET ENOUGH"

C oke frantically pulled the T-shirt over his head
and angrily stuffed it into a garbage can.

"Stupid! Stupid! Stupid!" he muttered. "How
could we have been so stupid as to trust that lady?
Mrs. Higgins is insane. She always has been. I should
have *known*!"

"I really thought she had changed," Pep said as
she put her Cubs shirt into the same trash can. "She
seemed so sad when she was talking about Dr. Warsaw. And she sounded so sincere when she was telling
us how unhappy she was working as a paid assassin."

"Sincere?" Coke sputtered. "She played us for fools."

"Do you think she was really in love with Dr. Warsaw? Do you think she was really going to marry him?" Pep asked. "Or was that a lie too?"

"Who knows?" Coke replied. "The two of them were made for each other. They're both psychos."

The twins debated whether or not Mrs. Higgins could be working together with Archie Clone, but they were interrupted when Coke's cell phone rang. As expected, it was their dad.

"Are you kids okay?" Dr. McDonald asked urgently. "Why did you say there was a bomb in the Cubs dugout? Are you crazy?"

"Yes, we're okay," Coke replied. "I don't know why we said there was a bomb in the Cubs dugout. Maybe we *are* crazy."

Dr. McDonald instructed the twins to meet him at a parking lot on North Sheffield Avenue, and hung up abruptly.

It took the twins awhile to retrace their steps and find the location. When they did, their father was leaning against the side of the RV, hands on hips. Never a good sign.

"If it was *so* important for you to leave the game early, you could have just said so," Dr. McDonald said sternly. "You didn't have to have them evacuate the whole ballpark."

"That wasn't it, Dad!" Pep replied. "Really! We would never do something like that."

"Then why did you do it?"

Pep looked at her brother, who was always better in situations like this.

"Dad," he began, "would you believe me if I said our health teacher Mrs. Higgins works for the Cubs now, and she told us that singing the last line of 'Take Me Out to the Ball Game' would trigger a bomb in the Cubs dugout? Dad, she put a gun to our heads and *forced* us to sing it."

"No," said Dr. McDonald. "I wouldn't believe that."

"What if we told you it was a chocolate gun?" added Pep.

"That was a very dangerous stunt!" their father scolded them. "People could have been killed running for the exits like that!"

"But if there really *was* a bomb in the Cubs dugout," Coke explained, "people really would have been killed!"

"But there *was* no bomb in the dugout!" Dr. McDonald shouted. "You did it for no reason at all!"

He shook his head and pinched the bridge of his nose between two fingers, which is what parents do for some reason when their kids do incomprehensibly dumb things.

They climbed into the RV and headed downtown on Michigan Avenue, where Mrs. McDonald had arranged to meet them. She was waiting when they pulled over to the curb across the street from Millennium Park.

"So how was the game?" Mrs. McDonald said cheerfully as she climbed into the front seat with a shopping bag.

None of them, not even Dr. McDonald, particularly wanted to go over what had happened at Wrigley Field.

"It was very exciting, Mom," Coke finally said.

"That must have been cool, seeing your names up on the video screen," Mrs. McDonald said. "Was it fun singing 'Take Me Out to the Ball Game'? That was my idea."

"It was a unique experience, Mom," Pep said diplomatically.

Dr. McDonald shook his head slightly and snorted to himself as he put the RV into gear. The streets were busy, but he managed to merge onto Lake Shore Drive and the Chicago Skyway—Route 90.

It was late afternoon by this time. Mrs. McDonald punched their location into the GPS. She did some rough calculations in her head as they left Chicago. It was June 26. They were about seven hundred miles from Washington, and they hoped to get there at least one day early to explore the capital before Aunt Judy's wedding on July Fourth. So they had about seven days to travel seven hundred miles. About a hundred miles a day. That was reasonable.

700

Go to Google Maps (http://maps.google .com/).

Click Get Directions.

In the A box, type Chicago IL.

In the B box, type Gary IN.

Click Get Directions.

They were making good time, and Dr. McDonald relaxed a little behind the wheel, brainstorming about his next book.

Maybe I should write a biography, he said to himself. *I've never done a biography. I could write about a historical figure. Maybe a president. People like to read biographies of presidents. . . .*

Dr. and Mrs. McDonald were both thankful that up until this point, they hadn't encountered any of the typical road trip calamities—lost wallets, mechanical failures, kids getting poison ivy, and so on.

(Little did they know that so far their children had been forced to jump off a cliff, locked in a burning school, pushed into a sand pit, thrown into a vat of

SPAM, zapped with electric shocks, lowered into boiling oil, and chased through the streets of Chicago by enraged Cub fans.)

Dr. McDonald knocked wood—well, the dashboard, anyway—and reached into the glove compartment to put on a CD—Michael Jackson's *Number Ones*. There was little the whole family could agree on, especially when it came to music. But after Michael Jackson died, they had all gone to see his concert film *This Is It*. By the time the movie was over the McDonalds had become Jackson fans. Four heads were bobbing together when the first notes to "Don't Stop 'Til You Get Enough" pumped out of the RV speakers.

"Oh, I almost forgot," Mrs. McDonald said suddenly. "I got you kids souvenirs."

She opened her shopping bag and pulled out a Cubs shirt for each of the twins. They immediately flipped them over to see if there was any writing on the back.

"Thanks, Mom!" Coke and Pep said together.

"I thought these would help you remember your day at Wrigley Field," Mrs. McDonald said.

"Oh, we'll remember our day at Wrigley Field," Pep said. "I'm sure of that."

They continued along Route 90 for a few miles when, at the same time, all four spotted a sign at the side of the road.

"Wooooooooo-hooooooooooooo!" Coke yelled. "Hey, do you know that five vice presidents were born in Indiana?"

"How can you possibly know that?" asked Pep.

"I read it on the place mat in a restaurant when we were in Wyoming," Coke said. "In fact, Indiana is nicknamed 'Mother of Vice Presidents.'"

"You're laboring under the misconception that anybody cares," Pep said.

The McDonalds couldn't see it, but they were only a mile from Lake Michigan at this time. "Billie Jean" pumped out of the RV speakers as Dr. McDonald pulled off Route 90 at exit 14B. The sign said GARY. He drove a couple of miles through this busy working-class city before the kids noticed they were no longer on the highway.

"What are we doing here?" Coke asked.

"Do either of you know what Gary, Indiana, is famous for?" asked Mrs. McDonald.

"I do!" Pep said excitedly. She began to sing that old song from *The Music Man* that consists mainly of the words "Gary, Indiana" repeated over and over again.

If you don't believe me, YouTube it.

"Nope, that's not it," Dr. McDonald said as he turned onto a street filled with very small houses. "Guess again."

"I give up," Coke said.

The RV stopped in front of a simple little house with white siding and a dark shingled roof.

"Look at the street sign on the corner," Mrs. McDonald said.

The sign said 2300 JACKSON STREET in one direction and JACKSON FAMILY BLVD in the other.

"Beat It" was pumping out of the RV speakers.

"This was Michael Jackson's house!" Pep yelled.

"That's right," Mrs. McDonald said. "It's his boyhood home."

Only then did the kids notice a few stuffed animals and flowers that fans had left near the front door.

Mrs. McDonald rolled down the window and snapped a few photos.

"Weren't there something like ten brothers and sisters in the Jackson family?" Coke asked. "And they all lived in this tiny little house?"

"Nine," Mrs. McDonald said. "The family moved to California when Michael was eleven."

"Is this a museum or something?" Pep asked. "Can we go inside?"

"No, somebody lives here," Dr. McDonald said.

"But this is like going to Graceland if you're an Elvis fan," Mrs. McDonald explained. "Like going to Liverpool if you're a Beatles fan. Like going to Hoboken if you're a Sinatra fan."

"Hoboken?" Coke asked. "What's that?"

"What's a Sinatra?" asked Pep.

"Forget it."

They listened to "Thriller" as they headed back onto the highway. Just ten miles east of Gary, they pulled into Yogi Bear's Jellystone Park Camp-Resort in Portage, Indiana. Mrs. McDonald had called ahead on her cell phone and made a reservation.

Dr. McDonald hooked the RV up to the camp's electrical system while the others pitched in to prepare dinner—frozen chicken and vegetables. Afterward, there was a campfire going on, and the kids went over to toast some marshmallows.

While they were sitting there, sticks in the fire, Coke was thinking about what had happened that day, and he suddenly remembered something. Back at Wrigley Field, right after their birthday message flashed up on the video screen, it had been replaced by another message. He had almost forgotten all about it, but his brain somehow had memorized the message itself.

Pep ran back to the RV to get her notebook so they could write it down and figure it out.

˥⊃⌐⌐⌐∧⊃⌐‹‹ ˥⊓⌐⊡⊐

"It looks like it might be some ancient picture language," Coke guessed. "Like something the Aztecs used, or the Egyptians."

"Or each of those symbols might represent a letter of the alphabet," Pep said.

Using the flickering light from the campfire, Pep puzzled over the strange symbols for a long time while Coke toasted more marshmallows. He had no patience for ciphers or puzzles, or any of that spy stuff his sister loved so much.

There were fourteen symbols, and numbers one and ten were the same. None of the others were repeated. Pep turned it upside down and sideways, trying to get a different perspective on it. The dots had to be important, or they wouldn't be there.

After a half hour or so, Pep called it quits. It was late. The fire was dying out, and it was getting hard to see the notebook. They were both tired. Most of the people staying at the campground had gone to sleep. She could work on it some more the next day.

Chapter 8

CRUISING INDIANA

As it turned out, Pep didn't have to work on the cipher the next day after all. While she was sleeping, her unconscious mind was working feverishly on the problem. The brain has a funny way of doing that. It *never* sleeps. And when Pep woke up in the morning, the solution was waiting for her.

"It's in Pigpen!" she whispered to her brother, who was still sleeping peacefully.

"Huh?" he muttered. "What?"

"That cipher we saw on the video screen at Wrigley Field yesterday," she whispered. "It's written in a code called Pigpen. I learned about it in Girl Scouts when I was little. They used it back in the eighteenth century to keep messages private."

"Whatever you say," Coke said, wiping his eyes.

Their parents were still asleep. Pep got out her notebook and explained to Coke how the code worked.

"Each of those symbols represents one letter, but we have to make a Pigpen grid to find out what the letters are. Let me see if I still remember how to make the grid."

She turned to the page with the cipher.

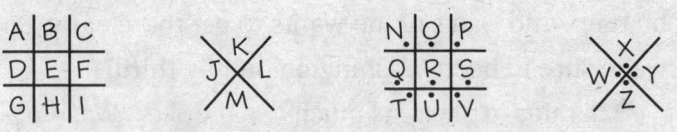

Then, directly below it, she wrote out a Pigpen grid as she remembered it.

"Look, the first symbol represents the letter *T*," Pep whispered. "See?"

Coke scanned the grid and saw that the little box with the *T* inside it matched the first symbol of the cipher.

"So that would mean that the second letter has to be . . . *W*," he whispered.

"Right," replied Pep. "And the third letter is *O*. So

that's probably the first word of the message—TWO."

After that, they were easily able to figure out the rest of the letters one by one—PMJULYTHIRD.

"Two o'clock in the afternoon on July third!" Pep whispered excitedly. "That's the message!"

Coke looked at his cell phone to check the date— June 27.

"July third is . . . six days from now," he said, counting them off.

"Something is going to happen at two o'clock on July third," said Pep.

"But that just tells us *when*," Coke whispered, "it doesn't tell us what's going to happen, or where."

"Aunt Judy's wedding will be the next day, on July Fourth," Pep said. "We'll have to be in Washington by then, and Dad said he wants to get there early. So we're sure to be in Washington on July third."

"That doesn't help us much," said Coke. "Washington is a big city."

"What are you two whispering about?" Dr. McDonald suddenly called out.

"Nothing, Dad!" Coke said. "Go back to sleep."

After everyone was awake, bathed, and breakfasted, the grown-ups huddled at the picnic table, poring over the laptop screen and road atlas.

"Family meeting!" Dr. McDonald announced, gathering everyone around him. "We have a big day ahead of us. My goal is to get across the great state of Indiana."

Dr. Ben McDonald was the kind of person who liked to set goals and achieve them. It gave him a feeling of satisfaction to cross things off his to-do list, and he tried to communicate the importance of setting goals to his children.

The plan for the day was to drive about a hundred fifty miles across northern Indiana, hitting five or six sites along the way that Mrs. McDonald could use in *Amazing but True*. They would start out on Route 80, which almost touches the Michigan border. At a certain point, they would veer off to visit some of the interesting sites south of the highway. He and Mrs. McDonald had mapped out the route carefully so they would stop at some historical sites for him, some offbeat sites for her, and also some sites that would keep the kids interested.

"Okay," Mrs. McDonald said, "first, let's go over the places we are *not* going to visit today. We are not going to see the world's largest toilet bowl in Columbus, Indiana."

"Oh, man!" Coke complained. "I really wanted to go there. In more ways than one."

"Very funny," Pep said.

"It's two hundred miles south of here, and we're heading east," Dr. McDonald explained.

200

"There's a twenty-foot statue of a woman made out of hubcaps in Jeffersonville," Mrs. McDonald continued, "but that's even farther south. And as much as I would love to see the world's largest ball of paint, it would be a three-hour drive to Alexandria."

"How big is the ball of paint?" Pep asked.

"It's over three thousand pounds," Mrs. McDonald said, consulting her guidebook. "Oh, and the world's largest hairball is not far from here. It's bigger than a basketball."

"Let's go!" Coke shouted.

"It's not on display anymore," Mrs. McDonald said.

"Bummer!"

"How was it possible for a cat to cough up a hairball bigger than a basketball, Mom?" Pep asked.

"It must have been a *very* large cat," Coke guessed.

"It was a cow," Mrs. McDonald said.

"Oh."

"The Santa Claus Museum in Santa Claus, Indiana, would be a five-hour drive," Dr. McDonald informed everyone, "and I refuse to go to Jones, Michigan, where your mother tells me there is a fake ghost town created by the guy who invented Kitty Litter. You'll just have to come back on another trip to see those places—preferably after I'm dead."

"So where are we going today?" asked Pep.

"Our first stop is the Lunkquarium," Mrs. McDonald replied.

"The *what*?!"

They checked out of the campground and headed east for about an hour on Route 80. Then Dr. McDonald pulled off exit 83, and a mile or so down the road a sign came into view:

Go to Google Maps (http://maps.google.com/).

Click Get Directions.

In the A box, type Portage IN.

In the B box, type Edwardsburg MI.

Click Get Directions.

"Michigan?" Pep asked. "What are we doing here, Dad? I thought you said we were going to cross Indiana today."

"We are," Dr. McDonald replied. "This is just a quick side trip."

"Woooooo-hooooooooo!" Coke hollered. "Did you know that Michigan is sometimes called the Wolverine State, even though there are no wolverines in Michigan anymore?"

"Get a life, brainiac," Pep told her brother.

Soon they arrived in Edwardsburg, which bills itself as the "Live Bait Capital of the World." Dr. McDonald pulled the RV into the big parking lot of a store called Lunker's. There was a giant rotating fish on the roof.

"I don't get it," Coke said as they walked through the front door. "It's a big fishing store."

But actually, it was much more. The ceiling of the store was painted blue with white clouds, to make it seem like you were in the great outdoors. Besides all the fishing and hunting gear, the store featured a stuffed bear, an alligator, some huge iguanas, an enormous aquarium (the Lunkquarium), and an eight-thousand-pound sculpture of a bass that looked like it was crashing through a brick wall.

Even Coke had to admit the place was cool.

Everybody had pretzels at the in-store restaurant before piling back into the RV.

"Okay, what's next, Mom?" asked Pep.

"Our next stop is the RV Hall of Fame," Mrs. McDonald announced.

"No!" Coke hollered. "It can't be true! They can't have a Hall of Fame devoted to RVs. Say it ain't so, Dad!"

But it was so. In Elkhart, Indiana, just eleven miles south of Lunker's, is the RV Hall of Fame. Mrs. McDonald read from the website.

> *Dedicated to preserving the history and honoring the pioneers and individuals who have made significant contributions to the RV and Manufactured Housing industries . . .*

"Bor-ing!" Coke shouted.

"Please, Mom!" Pep begged. "Don't make us go there. We'll go anywhere else you want. Just don't make us go *there*."

"Okay! Okay!" Mrs. McDonald agreed. "Stay on the road, Ben. We'll skip the RV Hall of Fame."

In the back, Coke and Pep breathed sighs of relief. They weren't sure if they would rather jump off a cliff, get locked in a burning building, or visit the RV Hall of Fame.

Go to Google Maps
(http://maps.google
.com/).

Click Get Directions.

In the A box, type
Edwardsburg MI.

In the B box, type
Mentone IN.

Click Get Directions.

"Next stop," Mrs. McDonald announced cheerfully. "The world's largest egg!"

It may be hard to believe, dear reader. But about an hour south of the RV Hall of Fame, in the little town of Mentone, Indiana, rests the largest egg in the world.

Well, it's not a real egg. And it may not even be the largest *fake* egg in the world, because there are other fake eggs in Washington State and Canada that the locals claim to be the largest.

But if you walk down Main Street in Mentone, you will almost surely see a three-thousand-pound, ten-foot-tall concrete egg standing on its end near a bank parking lot.

The twins were not in a position to beg off going to

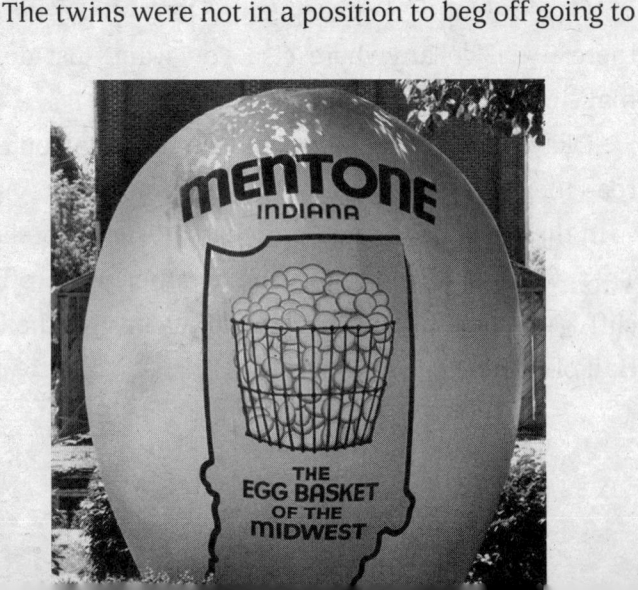

look at the giant egg, as they had already talked their parents into skipping the RV Hall of Fame. One should choose one's battles carefully.

"This is *it*?" Dr. McDonald asked as he walked up to the egg, somewhat disappointed.

"What do you mean, Ben?" the easily impressed Mrs. McDonald enthused. "This is *amazing*! How many people can say they saw the largest egg in the world in person?"

Dr. McDonald shook his head and went back to wait for the rest of the family in the RV.

"It's really not that big, Mom," Pep said. "And it's not even an egg. It's an egg-shaped object."

"I don't think this egg is as big as the world's largest ball of twine," Coke noted.

"You're comparing apples and oranges," Mrs. McDonald told him.

"No I'm not," Coke said. "I'm comparing balls of twine and fake eggs. If you want me to compare the world's largest apple and the world's largest orange . . ."

Mrs. McDonald ignored him, taking some photos and notes for her website.

"It's probably bigger than that hairball you told us about," Pep guessed, hoping to make her mother feel like it hadn't been a wasted trip.

"I can't believe we passed up the world's largest

toilet bowl to see *this*," Coke complained. "Let's blow this pop stand."

So they did. There's only so much time you can spend looking at a gigantic concrete egg.

"What's next, Mom?" asked Pep as they drove out of Mentone.

"Oh, you're going to like *this*," she replied mysteriously.

Thirty miles directly south of Mentone, on the banks of the Wabash River, is the town of Peru, Indiana. Peru is called the "Circus Capital of the World," because it used to be the winter home of Ringling Brothers and other circuses. But the McDonald family didn't come to Peru to see lions or tigers or bears.

They came to see a pair of pants.

"Do you kids remember a couple of days ago, when Dad and I went to that shoe store in Illinois to see the shoes of the tallest man in the world?" Mrs. McDonald asked as they turned onto North Broadway in Peru.

"Yeah."

"Well, his pants are here."

Coke and Pep looked at each other as their dad pulled into the parking lot at Miami County Museum.

Go to Google Maps (http://maps.google.com/).

Click Get Directions.

In the A box, type Mentone IN.

In the B box, type Peru IN.

Click Get Directions.

"We came here to see a pair of *pants*?" Coke asked. "You gotta be kidding me."

"Well, they're overalls actually," Mrs. McDonald replied.

They went inside the museum and looked all over for an extremely large pair of overalls.

"Hey, check this out," Coke said as he spotted a giant skull. "Maybe this is that guy's head."

In fact, the skull was labeled "Big Charley the Killer Elephant." Apparently, Big Charley was a circus elephant that got mad at his trainer one day in 1901 and drowned him. So Big Charley was shot, and his skull was put in the museum. The bullet holes were plainly visible.

"That's gross," Pep said, with obvious fascination.

Mrs. McDonald took some photos and notes for *Amazing but True*. But not far from the giant skull, she found what she was looking for.

"Feast your eyes," she told the family, "and behold . . . the pants . . . of the tallest man in the world!"

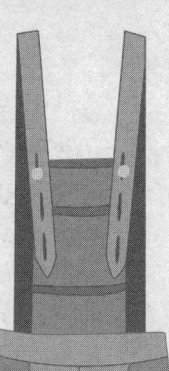

There they were. The pants belonged to Robert Wadlow, the Illinois man whose body produced too much growth hormone. When he was thirteen years old, the sign on the wall said, he was seven feet four inches tall. At age twenty-two, he was eight feet eleven inches tall.

"Those are some *big* pants," Dr. McDonald admitted.

"That guy must have been some basketball player," Coke marveled.

"Actually, he could barely stand up," Mrs. McDonald said. "He died when he was just twenty-two, in 1940."

"That's sad," Pep said quietly.

"Okay, can we get out of here now?" asked Coke. "This place is creepy."

Mrs. McDonald insisted on stopping in the gift shop before leaving. She gave each of the kids money to get a souvenir. Pep bought a book about circus animals, and Coke bought a can of Silly String.

By the time the McDonalds got out of the museum, it was afternoon. They still had a long way to go to get through

Go to Google Maps (http://maps.google.com/).

Click Get Directions.

In the A box, type Peru IN.

In the B box, type Huntington IN,

Click Get Directions.

Indiana. So it was quick ham and cheese sandwiches in the RV and back on the road, heading
east along Route 24 thirty-five miles to the town of
Huntington. That's where they saw this sign:

Visit
THE DAN QUAYLE
VICE PRESIDENT
MUSEUM

"No!" Coke hollered from the back. "Not another
museum!"

"Do we have to go?" asked Pep. "I never even heard
of Dan Quayle."

"Calm down," Dr. McDonald told the kids. "We're
not taking you to another museum."

Instead, he pulled into the Tel-Hy Nature Preserve.
The kids assumed they would be observing nature,
but Dr. McDonald drove down the road a bit until he
stopped in front of a row of little shacks.

"It's *amazing*!" said Mrs. McDonald.

"I give up," Coke said. "What is it?"

"Back in 1960," Mrs. McDonald informed them, "a
couple named Hy and Lorry Goldenberg bought an
outhouse for three dollars. They liked it so much that
they started collecting outhouses. When Hy died,

Lorry donated seventeen of them here. It's probably the largest collection of outhouses in the world!"

"It's also probably the *only* collection of outhouses in the world," Dr. McDonald commented.

The outhouses were lined up in a row, and the family examined most of them. One of them seated three people at a time, which must have been interesting. Mrs. McDonald took photos and notes.

"Fascinating," said Dr. McDonald. "Let's get out of here."

The grave site of Johnny Appleseed was only thirty miles away near Fort Wayne, but Mrs. McDonald decided to skip it, because there is some dispute over where Mr. Appleseed is actually buried. Instead, they headed north on Route 3 to Kendallville, home of the Mid-America Windmill Museum.

Go to Google Maps (http://maps.google.com/).

Click Get Directions.

In the A box, type Huntington IN.

In the B box, type Kendallville IN.

Click Get Directions.

"No!" Coke screamed. "Not another museum! I'll *die* if I have to visit another museum."

"Someday," Dr. McDonald lectured him, "wind power, solar power, and other forms of renewable energy will replace coal, oil, and gas. You kids should learn about this stuff."

Dr. McDonald had a special interest in the subject, having authored *The Impact of Coal on the Industrial Revolution*.

"Can't Pep and I just stay in the RV?" Coke begged.

"Fine!" Dr. McDonald said.

By the way, anytime someone says a sentence that consists of just the word "fine," they mean the exact opposite of fine. The situation is *not* fine, and they are not happy about it.

Mrs. McDonald insisted on locking the doors of the RV, just to be on the safe side.

"Don't worry about us, Mom," Coke said. "We can take care of ourselves."

The grown-ups went off to tour the windmill museum. Coke listened to his iPod, while Pep worked on a crossword puzzle. After about fifteen minutes, she suddenly looked up.

"I have a bad feeling," she said.

Coke took off one earbud so he could hear her.

"What?"

"Somebody's out there," Pep told him. "I have a feeling."

They both looked out the windows. Nobody was around. It was just a parking lot, and there were no other vehicles in it.

"It's nothing," Coke told his sister. "You're paranoid."

But in fact it wasn't nothing, because ten minutes later a black pickup truck pulled into the parking lot and stopped about twenty yards away. A man wearing a baseball cap got out.

"Look!" Pep shouted.

The twins got out of their seats and crept to the window, keeping their heads low.

"Is it Archie Clone?" Coke asked.

"No," Pep replied, "and it's not one of the bowler dudes either. This guy is too big. I've never seen him before."

The guy in the baseball cap rooted around in the back of his truck for about five minutes, like he was trying to find something. Then he pulled something out.

A chain saw.

"He's got a *chain saw*!" Coke yelled, grabbing his sister.

"So what?"

"Didn't you ever see *The Texas Chain Saw Massacre*?" Coke said. "A lunatic named Leatherface murders a bunch of people with a chain saw!"

"Ahhhhhhhhhhhhhhhhhhh!" both twins screamed.

The guy with the chain saw was walking slowly toward the RV.

"Help! Help!" Pep shouted. "What are we gonna do?"

"We're gonna die!" moaned Coke. "He's gonna tear our limbs off!"

The guy with the chain saw was getting closer.

And closer.

"This is it," Pep said, sobbing uncontrollably. "We're trapped in here. There's no way out!"

"It's all over," Coke said, trying his best not to break down. "I never thought it would end this way. Oh no, he's almost here! Here he comes!"

And then the guy with the chain saw walked past the RV without stopping. He opened the door to a shed on the side of the museum and went inside.

Coke and Pep collapsed on the floor of the RV, panting and sweating.

"I guess he's going to cut down a tree," Pep said.

"Yeah, probably."

A few minutes later, their parents came out of the windmill museum.

"Oh, you kids missed a good time," Mrs. McDonald said. "We learned all about windmills."

"Anything exciting happen while we were gone?" asked Dr. McDonald.

"Nah," Coke said, "except for the psycho who almost attacked us with a chain saw."

"Ha, ha, you kids crack me up."

Dr. and Mrs. McDonald felt a little guilty going to

the museum while the kids sat in the RV. They had talked it over and agreed that the next day they would do something just for the kids.

The McDonalds followed Route 6 out of Kendall-ville, heading east. After twenty-five miles, they came to this.

"We did it!" Dr. McDonald shouted. "We made it all the way across Indiana in one day!"

"Woooo-hooooo!" roared Coke. "The Buckeye State!"

"What's a buckeye?" Pep asked.

"It's a kind of tree," Coke told her. "Hey, I bet you guys can't name four things that were invented in Ohio."

"I know that Thomas Edison and the Wright

Brothers were born in Ohio," Dr. McDonald said.

"Yes, but they were inventors, not inventions," Coke said.

"Go ahead," groaned Pep. "You know you want to tell us."

"The traffic light, the cash register, chewing gum, and hot dogs!" Coke yelled.

"How can you possibly know that?" his sister asked.

"It's all up here, baby," Coke said, pointing to his forehead.

They crossed the Ohio state line and drove another ten miles

before heading south on Route 127. The sun was dipping lower toward the horizon. Everybody was getting hungry for dinner.

Go to Google Maps (http://maps.google.com/).

Click Get Directions.

In the A box, type Kendallville IN.

In the B box, type Paulding OH.

Click Get Directions.

After fifteen miles, they reached the town of Paulding and pulled into Woodbridge Campground. The kids were relieved that it wasn't one of those bare-bones places with nothing to do but eat and sleep. A sign said there was bingo on Friday night, a horseshoe tournament on Saturday afternoon, and lots of other stuff to do.

Dr. McDonald went to check in at the office and get a newspaper so he could see what was happening in the world. Mrs. McDonald started preparing dinner. Coke noticed a tetherball court, and he and Pep went over there to hit the ball back and forth.

It had been a good day, all in all. For the McDonald twins, any day in which nobody tried to kill them was a good day.

In fact, it had been *two* days since there had been an attempt on their lives. Unless, of course, you were to count those angry Cubs fans who chased them out of Wrigley Field. But nobody had tried to kill them at Michael Jackson's house. Nobody tried to kill them at the Lunkquarium, at the largest egg in the world, or at any of the places they had visited in Indiana. Maybe Bones and Mya had been right. They could relax a little until they got to Washington, D.C.

"Maybe we finally lost them," Pep said hopefully as she whacked the tetherball over Coke's head.

"I doubt it," Coke replied, remembering the GPS chips that had been implanted in their skulls.

Mrs. McDonald called everyone to dinner—some kind of anonymous beefy stew that came from a bag in the freezer. It wasn't gourmet cuisine, but it was food. Afterward, the kids started a game of Scrabble while their parents relaxed on Adirondack chairs and read the newspaper. It was Pep who spotted the headline on the other side of the page her father was reading.

HERMAN WARSAW, DEAD AT 39

Prolific inventor and government researcher Dr. Herman Warsaw died yesterday at the age of 39. Dr. Warsaw, who made a fortune by inventing a GPS device to locate missing cats and dogs, went on to a second career consulting for the government and worked for one dollar per year at the Pentagon in Washington. He died from injuries sustained during a fall in Spring Green, Wisconsin, where he had been vacationing. The circumstances of the fall have not been disclosed. Dr. Warsaw had no known relatives.

Coke and Pep read the obituary twice, just to make sure they didn't miss a word.

"What are you kids staring at?" Dr. McDonald said. "Get your own newspaper if you want to read."

Coke pulled Pep over to the empty basketball court, where they could talk privately.

"So Dr. Warsaw is dead for sure," Coke said.

"And we killed him," said Pep. "That makes us murderers."

Tears welled up in her eyes. She felt no sympathy

for Dr. Warsaw, but the realization that they had actually caused another human being to die would be tough for anybody to handle.

"It was self-defense," Coke assured her, putting a hand on her shoulder. "We had to do it. He would have killed *us* if we didn't fight back."

There was a seesaw nearby, and each twin went over and sat on one end of it. It was time to take stock of their situation.

"What now?" Pep asked, not really expecting an answer.

Dr. Warsaw was dead, which was a good thing, of course. They wouldn't have to worry about that nut job anymore. But they *would* have to worry about Mrs. Higgins, who was very much alive. From her little performance at Wrigley Field, it seemed that she was crazier than ever. And if it was true that Dr. Warsaw was the love of her life, she would be all the more motivated to track Coke and Pep down and get revenge. She had said it herself—she was going to make their lives a living hell.

"If Dr. Warsaw is dead," Pep asked, "who do you think has been sending us those ciphers?"

"Could be the bowler dudes," Coke guessed.

Pep had almost forgotten about the lunatics who wore bowler hats. They were the ones who'd chased them over the cliff, and they were the ones who had thrown them into the pit at Sand Mountain. The last time they showed their faces, it was at The House on the Rock, when they'd dressed up in suits of armor and dragged both twins to The Infinity Room. But the bowler dudes didn't seem bright enough to create ciphers.

"Mya or Bones could have sent the last one," Pep said. "Maybe they're trying to contact us."

"Or it could be Archie Clone," Coke suggested, recalling the red-haired teenage maniac who'd tried to drown them in boiling oil at McDonald's. "Remember, he wants all The Genius Files kids dead so he can collect a million dollars when he turns twenty-one."

"We can't let down our guard," Pep warned. "As soon as we relax, that's when they're going to strike again."

Coke snapped his fingers.

"I think I know why nobody tried to kill us in Indiana," he said.

"Why?"

"Because they're on their way to Washington," he replied. "It's obvious. They know we're going there."

Pep thought it over and agreed that her brother was probably right. Why should anyone bother chasing them to every giant egg or hairball in the Midwest?

He or she could just go to Washington and do the job there. All the people who were trying to kill them knew they were going to their aunt's wedding in Washington.

"In other words, we're walking right into a trap," she said.

Coke and Pep had things figured out pretty well. But they were wrong about one minor detail. Whoever was trying to kill them was *not* going to Washington to do it there.

No, they were going to do it in Ohio.

Chapter 9
NEVER ARGUE WITH A GROWN-UP

Long after their parents went to sleep, Coke and Pep were still sitting on a bench outside the RV, whispering in the dark.

"We can't go to Washington," Coke said. "Mrs. Higgins or Archie Clone or those bowler dudes will be waiting for us. They may even be working together. We're playing right into their hands. It's a suicide mission."

"What do you think would happen if we didn't show up in Washington on July third?" Pep wondered. "What if we just turned around now and went home? Do you think they'd follow us?"

"I don't know," Coke said. "They seem pretty determined. But who knows? Maybe they'd just cross us off their list of Genius Files kids and move on to the next name."

"They have lots of other kids to worry about," Pep said hopefully. "Dr. Warsaw told us there were hundreds of kids in The Genius Files program."

"The odds are sure to be better for us if we went home than if we continued on to Washington," said Coke. "And if they *did* come after us in California, at least we'd have home field advantage."

"But how are we going to talk Mom and Dad into letting us go home?" Pep asked. "Every time we tell them that people are trying to kill us, they think we're just joking."

"Leave it to me," Coke replied. "I can talk Dad into *anything*."

It was after midnight when the twins finally went to bed. In the morning, Mrs. McDonald made some eggs on the little stove in the RV and toasted some English muffins. It was a rare treat. Usually, breakfast on the road was cold cereal.

After they cleaned up the dishes, Coke and Pep pulled their father off to the side, near the volleyball court.

"Dad," Coke said very seriously, "we need to talk to you about something."

"Is everything okay?" Dr. McDonald asked, concerned.

"Everything's fine," Coke said quietly. "But . . . we want to turn back. We want to go home."

"What?!" Dr. McDonald asked, surprised. "Why? This is a great vacation. Aren't you kids having fun?"

"Sure we are, Dad," Pep said. "It's just that . . ."

"We're homesick," Coke said.

Coke had decided to play the homesick card. Parents are suckers for homesickness. It means your kids like being home so much that nowhere else compares. It means you must be a terrific parent to have raised wonderful kids who like being in your house. It means you have created a lovely atmosphere for your children. It pulls at the heartstrings. Home is where the heart is. Home sweet home.

A kid can't miss playing the homesick card.

"I miss my friends," Pep added, with her best puppy-dog face.

"And I have a ton of summer reading to do," Coke said. "I'm worried that I won't be able to finish it before school starts up again."

"We just want to go home," Pep said.

The McDonald twins were not lying. They *were*

homesick. They *did* miss their friends. They *had* summer reading assignments. It might not have been the *whole* truth, but telling their parents the whole truth hadn't worked. So it was time to try a different strategy. Pep's watery eyes were not filled with fake tears.

Dr. McDonald put an arm around each of his children.

"Kids," he said, "do you know how far we've traveled on this trip? More than two *thousand* miles. That's a *long* way. Right now we're only about five hundred miles from Washington. We've come so far."

"We know, Dad," Coke said. "But—"

"Don't you want to see the nation's capital?" Dr. McDonald continued. "The Lincoln Memorial? The Washington Monument? The White House? The Smithsonian? Believe me, you're going to remember the things that happened on this trip for the rest of your lives."

"I'll say," Coke agreed.

"But Dad—," Pep said before her father cut her off.

"Tell me, what do you think would have happened if Thomas Edison had tried just a few filaments for his lightbulb and said, 'Ah, forget it. It's not worth the effort. Candles give off enough light'?"

"We'd still be using candles today," Pep guessed.

"That's right!" her father said.

Dr. McDonald was using the time-honored "what if" strategy. Kids are suckers for the "what if" strategy. The parent makes outlandish comparisons with the current situation, and the kids don't realize the two situations are totally different. It works every time.

"What if," Dr. McDonald asked, "Lewis and Clark had stopped in the middle of Iowa and said, 'Okay, we get the idea. We've seen enough amber waves of grain and purple mountain majesties'? And what if Neil Armstrong had stopped halfway to the moon and decided that one small half step for man was good enough? And what if Magellan had turned back when he was halfway around the world?"

"He would have survived, Dad," Coke said. "Magellan died before he could circle the globe. He was murdered in the Philippines."

"You know what I mean," Dr. McDonald said. "The point is that you don't start a job and quit in the middle. That's just not right. And it's not the American way. If you start something, you should finish it."

Coke had a pained look on his face. This wasn't going at all as he had planned. He hadn't counted on his dad pulling the old "what if" strategy right after he played the homesick card. He didn't know what to say next.

That was the problem with arguing against parents. They had so much more experience at it. Coke had to try something else. Desperate times call for desperate measures.

"Dad," he said, "I don't feel very well. It's my stomach. I didn't want to ruin the trip for everybody, but I think it's cancer. I'm probably dying. I need to go home and spend my final days there."

Yes! *Nothing* tops the old "I'm dying" trick.

"Wait a minute," Dr. McDonald said, taking his arm off Coke's shoulder. "First you said you need to go home to do your summer reading, and *now* you say you have to go home because you're *dying*?"

"I really want to finish my summer reading before I die," Coke explained. "Like you said, it's the American way to finish what you started."

At that point, Mrs. McDonald came ambling over.

"What's going on?" she asked. "It's time to get this show on the road. I'm anxious to see Ohio."

"The kids say they don't want to go to Washington," her husband said glumly. "They want to turn around and go home. Oh, and Coke thinks he's sick and he's going to die."

"Out of the question," Mrs. McDonald said immediately. "We can't go home now. Aunt Judy is my only sister. When we were little girls, we promised we would be at each other's wedding. She came to mine fourteen years ago, so I have to be there for hers. We *promised*. I haven't seen Judy in so long. I barely even remember what she looks like."

"What if you and Dad went to Aunt Judy's wedding, and Pep and I caught a flight home?" Coke suggested lamely. He knew he had lost the argument, but it was worth a try anyway.

"We're not sending you home alone," Mrs. McDonald said. "You're too young to be alone. The four of us are going to Washington. We're a family. That's all there is to it. End of story. And if you die, you're in big trouble, mister."

Mothers have a way of ending debates.

Silently, the twins climbed back into the RV. They would be going all the way to Washington, and they couldn't do anything about it. They would have to make the best of it.

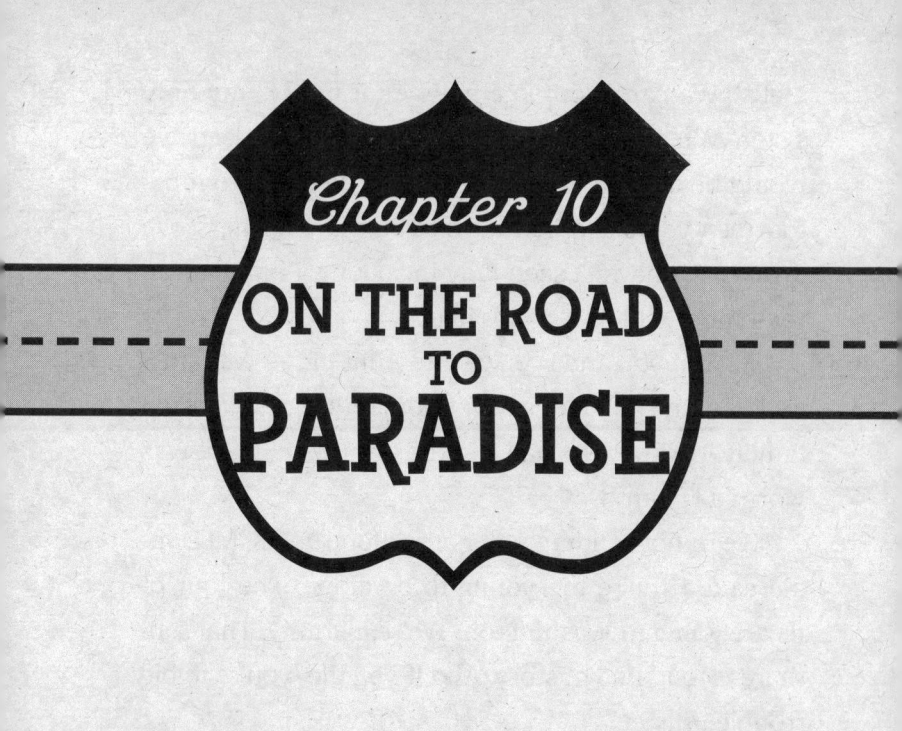

Chapter 10

ON THE ROAD
TO
PARADISE

O
hio is about two hundred fifty miles across.
It would be a *long* day. Pep opened her book
about circus animals. Coke fiddled with an
empty Pez dispenser, which his mother had bought
for him at the Museum of Pez Memorabilia back in
California. It reminded him of home.

"Where are we going now?" Coke asked glumly as
they pulled out of the campground's parking lot. "The
Pencil Sharpener Museum?"

"How did *you* know there was a pencil sharpener
museum in Ohio?" asked Mrs. McDonald.

"It was a lucky guess," Coke said, slipping the Pez dispenser into his back pocket.

"Well, I have good news for you," Mrs. McDonald announced. "We are *not* going to the Pencil Sharpener Museum. And we are not going to the Paperweight Museum, or the National Construction Equipment Museum, or the Merry-Go-Round Museum, or the Bicycle Museum of America, or the Annie Oakley museum, or even the Cardboard Boat Museum. Personally, I would love to visit all those wonderful Ohio landmarks."

"So where *are* we going?" Pep asked.

"Today we're going someplace just for *you*," Dr. McDonald told the kids. "We're going to Cedar Point!"

"Cedar Point?" Pep asked. "What kind of museum is that?"

"It sounds like the name of a mental institution," Coke remarked.

"Cedar Point happens to be the greatest amusement park in the *world*!" Dr. McDonald replied, grinning broadly. "And it's in Sandusky, Ohio!"

"Really?" Pep screamed, jumping out of her seat to wrap her arms around her parents. "I love you!"

Go to Google Maps (http://maps.google.com/).

Click Get Directions.

In the A box, type Paulding OH.

In the B box, type Toledo OH.

Click Get Directions.

There are great amusement parks in California, of course. Six Flags. Sea World. Disneyland. But Sandusky, Ohio, is almost sacred ground for roller-coaster fanatics around the world. Its first coaster was built back in 1892. Now Cedar Point is filled with them, and they are among the tallest and fastest in the world. Both of the twins loved thrill rides, the scarier the better.

Dr. McDonald popped a piece of gum into his mouth and an AC/DC disc into the CD player. It always amazed him that one of his favorite rock bands of his youth was also loved by his children.

"Turn it up!" Coke shouted over the music. He liked his music loud. The louder the better.

Dr. McDonald followed the local roads until he reached Route 24 East, which he stayed on for a long fifty-five miles. By that time, stomachs had started growling and it was decided unanimously to stop off for lunch well before they got to Cedar Point. It's not a good idea to ride a roller coaster on a full stomach.

Dr. McDonald pulled off the road at Toledo, where he saw a truck advertising a hot dog restaurant called Tony Packo's. BITE THE BEST, it said on the side of the truck. He couldn't resist.

"Holy Toledo!" Coke said as they walked into Tony Packo's.

The walls of the restaurant were covered with plaques, each one bearing a hot dog bun that had been autographed by a famous person. Jerry Seinfeld. George W. Bush. Bing Crosby. Patti LaBelle. Clint Black. There were five hundred of them.

"This place is like a hot dog bun museum!" Mrs. McDonald said, reaching for her camera. Tony Packo's would be perfect for *Amazing but True*.

They found an empty table and the waitress, an older woman, came over.

"What'll it be, folks?" she asked.

"Hot dogs!" all four replied.

"Good choice."

The kids walked around examining the autographed buns on the wall, but it wasn't long before their hot dogs arrived, so they rushed back to their table. Coke was about to bite into his hot dog when he decided to put some ketchup on it. As he opened up the bun, this is what he saw burned into it:

"Oh no," he said to himself. He quickly scanned the restaurant, then glanced over at the other buns on the table. Nobody else's bun had weird symbols burned into it.

Without saying a word, Coke showed the bun to his sister. She raised her eyebrows.

"Memorize it," Pep whispered in his ear.

"I already did."

The cipher committed to memory, Coke doused the dog with ketchup and destroyed the evidence, by eating it.

Back on the road to Cedar Point after lunch, the twins huddled together in the back of the RV as Coke wrote down the symbols he had seen on his hot dog bun.

"It's indecipherable!" he whispered.

"Every cipher is decipherable," Pep whispered back. "That's why they're called ciphers. And this one, actually, is *easily* decipherable. It uses the Ogham alphabet."

"The *what*?!"

"It was a medieval alphabet used in Ireland, Scotland, and Wales," she said, as she began writing it out.

"How can you possibly know that?" Coke asked.

"The same way you know worthless trivia like the four things that were invented in Ohio," she replied.

Pep finished writing out the Ogham alphabet.

"How do you decode it?" Coke asked.

"The first symbol, the two lines dropping straight down, represents the letter *G*," Pep said. "See? It's followed by an *R*. The next two letters are the same—*E*. After that is an *N*. So the first word is GREEN."

"No it's not," Coke whispered. He had already figured out the next five letters—SBORO. "The first word is GREENSBORO."

Together, they figured out the next five letters—LUNCH. They puzzled over that for a moment before decoding the rest of the message—COUNTER.

GREENSBORO LUNCH COUNTER

"Does that mean anything to you?" Coke whispered to his sister.

"No," Pep replied.

"Yo, parental units!" Coke called out to the front of the RV. "If I say the words 'Greensboro lunch counter,' what comes to mind?"

"Greensboro, North Carolina, 1960," Dr. McDonald replied right away. "Four African American students sat at a lunch counter where only whites were allowed to sit. It was one of the defining moments of the civil rights movement."

"Are we going to North Carolina on this trip?" Pep whispered to her brother.

"I don't think so," he replied.

Coke and Pep looked at each other and shrugged.

"Why do you ask about the Greensboro lunch counter?" asked Dr. McDonald.

"Oh, we just decoded a secret message that had been burned into my hot dog bun," Coke replied. "It said 'Greensboro lunch counter.'"

"Very funny," Mrs. McDonald said. "You kids have such vivid imaginations."

Pep turned to a clean page in her notebook and started a list.

- July 3, two p.m.
- Greensboro lunch counter

"Maybe we'll get another cipher and it will all make sense," she whispered.

It was another fifty-five miles to Sandusky, on the shores of Lake Erie. The McDonalds pulled into the Cedar Point parking lot just before noon. Coke usually took his backpack with him wherever he went, but his mother told him to leave it in the RV. She didn't want to see it flying off a roller coaster.

While their parents waited in line to buy tickets, Coke and Pep looked around with wonder. There were seventeen roller coasters here, one of the largest collections in the world. Cedar Point also had fifteen thrill rides, a dozen water slides, parasailing, shows, music, and all the junk food you could eat. It was paradise.

Go to Google Maps (http://maps.google.com/).

Click Get Directions.

In the A box, type Toledo OH.

In the B box, type Sandusky OH.

Click Get Directions.

This would make up for everything they had endured to get here. For the first time in a long time, thoughts of evil health teachers, psychos wearing bowler hats, Archie Clone, and Dr. Herman Warsaw vanished from their minds.

"I think this place is heaven," Coke said in awe.

"Can we get ice cream?" Pep asked.

"Sure," Dr. McDonald agreed, "but don't you want to ride the roller coasters first?"

"Yeah!"

"I don't like being upside down," Mrs. McDonald announced. "I'm going to stick with the wimpy rides."

"I'll hang with Mom," said Dr. McDonald. "You kids go have fun. Keep in touch with us on your cell phones."

If you, dear reader, have been following The Genius Files closely, you may have noticed by now that whenever the twins go off on their own without their parents, someone tries to kill them. Uncanny, isn't it? Unfortunately, Coke and Pep have yet to notice this phenomenon. Foolishly, they waved good-bye and went off in search of thrills.

And they would find them.

The twins examined the park map to plan their amusement park strategy. If you're going to go to an amusement park, you have to have an amusement park strategy, right?

They would avoid all the kiddie rides and wimpy rides, of course. The thrill rides and water stuff would be fun to do, but Coke and Pep decided to hold off on them. If the lines were long, they might only get to a limited number of rides during the day. Cedar Point was famous for its coasters, so they should concentrate on them first. If there was time later, they could hit the other stuff. It was a solid plan.

The lines were manageable. First they rode the Corkscrew, which turns you upside down three times. Their brains fully scrambled, they got in line for the Top Thrill Dragster, which reaches speeds of 120 miles per hour. Hearts racing, they made their way to Millennium Force, which tops out at 310 feet up in the air. They survived Mantis, where you have to stand up the whole time. They did Gemini. They did Magnum XL-200. They were dizzy with euphoria.

As they were walking down the ramp after Magnum XL-200, Coke sent a text to his mom.

```
this is the gr8est day of my life
thanx for giving birth to me
```

"I hate to bring this up," Pep said as they headed for the next coaster, "but I have the feeling that somebody is following us."

"What?" Coke said. "Are you kidding me? There are thousands of people here. What could they do? And if somebody was going to try something, they would have made their move by now."

But Pep was usually right about her feelings. Coke looked around and scoped out the area. They were near another coaster, one called Disaster Transport. "Come on," he told Pep. "Let's duck in here."

There was no line at Disaster Transport, and soon the twins were sitting in the little car, getting seat-belted in by a teenage girl with a nose ring. The seat in front of theirs was empty. Coke glanced behind as a precaution. Nobody was sitting in that seat either. They were safe. The car was nestled in a U-shaped trough, sort of like a bobsled in the Olympics.

"Have fun!" the girl with the nose ring said as their car started inching forward.

The twins were in total darkness almost immediately, except for two rows of white lights on the left and right walls. Then the lights disappeared and they couldn't see a thing. The coaster took its first big dip, and Pep screamed. Coke held on tightly. In the dark, they couldn't tell when the next curve would be, or when the next plunge would be, and that was what made Disaster Transport so terrifying. The car went through a series of twisting turns, and then, suddenly, for no reason, it screeched to a halt.

They were sitting in total darkness, not moving. It looked something like this . . .

"What's going on?" Pep asked nervously.

"Relax," Coke told his sister. "This is probably part of the ride. They want you to think you'll be stuck here. I'm sure it will start up again in a few seconds."

It didn't.

Dark. Tunnel. Underground. Silence. Pep didn't like this situation.

"Do you think it's a mechanical problem?" she asked, looking all around to see if she could see a crack of light anywhere. Her eyes were starting to adjust to the dark. "We should tell somebody."

That's when she heard a muffled cough coming from the car behind them.

"Hello," two voices said pleasantly.

Pep thought frantically. Hadn't that car been empty when the ride started? How did those people get in there? Could they have possibly climbed in during the ride?

The two people in the car behind them pulled little flashlights out of their pockets and shined them upward at their own smiling faces.

They were men. One of them had a mustache. And both were wearing bowler hats.

"Eeeeeeeeeeeeeeeeeeeeeekkk!" Pep screamed. "The bowler dudes!"

"Holy !@#$%!" Coke exclaimed.

"Long time no see!" one of the bowler dudes said, a smile on his demented face. "Fancy meeting you two in here, of all places."

Pep screamed again as Coke frantically tried to remove his seat belt.

"Don't bother screaming, sweetheart," the mustachioed bowler dude said. "Nobody will notice. *Everybody* screams in here. That's why we decided this would be the perfect place."

"The perfect place for what?" Pep asked, not really wanting to hear the answer.

"The perfect place to kill you!"

"Hahahaha!" chortled the other bowler dude.

In the dark, Coke couldn't get his hands on the release button to his seat belt. The bowler dudes climbed out of their car and strolled over, as if they were taking a walk in the park.

"Eeeeeeeeeeeeeeeeeeeeekkk!" Pep screamed again.

"Help!" shouted Coke.

"Shut up!"

The bowler dudes pulled out long pocketknives and used them to cut through Coke's and Pep's seat belts. Then they pulled the twins to their feet.

"Get your hands off of me!" Coke shouted. "I'll call the cops on you!"

The bowler dudes laughed their cackling laugh, as if that was the funniest thing they had ever heard.

The twins were dragged through the dark tunnel for about ten yards until they reached a doorway. The bowler dudes pushed them through the door, across a short wooden walkway, and into another doorway that led to a dark room. There, they forced Coke and Pep into metal folding chairs and tied their arms behind their backs with rope.

"Have fun!" one of them said as he flipped a light on. Both of the bowler dudes went back out the door they had entered, cackling the whole time.

Coke and Pep looked around the small room. There were ice cream dispensers along the walls and posters with photos of ice cream pops on them. It didn't take a genius to figure out where they were.

In the back of a Mister Softee truck.

Chapter 11

I SCREAM.
YOU SCREAM.

The windows of the Mister Softee truck, where kids would ordinarily be standing in line to buy ice cream, were covered. It appeared to be dark outside, which seemed odd because it was the middle of the day. Suddenly, the Mister Softee theme song began to play.

"What are we doing in here?" Pep asked.

"How should I know?" Coke replied.

"I'll tell you what you're doing in here," a voice said from the front of the truck.

A chubby guy came out from the driver's seat. He

was wearing a white Mister Softee uniform, complete with the paper hat. When he pulled off the hat, his bright red hair could be seen.

"Archie Clone!" Coke shouted.

"No!" Pep yelled. "Not *him*!"

"Well, well, well," Archie Clone said, a smile on his face. "We meet again."

Coke struggled to pull his arms loose from the ropes, but there was no way to get them out.

"That was pretty clever, the way you used that Cheesehead to escape from my french fry simulator," Archie Clone continued.

"What do you want from us *now*?" Coke barked.

"The same thing I wanted from you last time," Archie Clone replied. "Your lives."

"You'll never get away with this," Pep told him, struggling to free her hands from the ropes. "Our parents are right outside."

"Parents!" Archie Clone said, with a snort. "Your parents think you're outside having a whole-some, carefree, and perfectly safe afternoon, Pep. It wouldn't occur to them in a million years that an amusement park is the *perfect* place to commit murder. I mean, think about it. A simple loose screw on a roller coaster. A sharp blade positioned at neck level for just a moment in a thrill ride. A *real* monster in the haunted house. It would be so easy! And nobody would ever know. There are frequently 'accidents' at amusement parks, if you know what I mean."

"If it's so easy, why didn't you do one of those things?" Coke asked.

"Oh, fatal roller coaster accidents are *so* cliché," Archie Clone said. "I prefer to do things my own way, Coke. This is how I express my creativity. Some people paint. Others make music or films. I'm a magician. Ha, ha! I make kids disappear. It's my *art*."

The twins could hardly believe what they were hearing. If Archie Clone hadn't proven his insanity at their first meeting, he was proving it now. It was possible that he might be even crazier than Dr. Warsaw was.

"Tell me something," he said. "You kids like ice cream, don't you?"

"Why do *you* care?" Pep shouted defiantly.

"Pep, I wish you wouldn't be so angry with me all the time," Archie Clone said soothingly. "I just want to give you some ice cream. I thought we were friends."

"Over my dead body!" she shouted back.

"Precisely!"

Coke looked around for a weapon, a tool, anything he could use to get out of this situation. He wished he had his backpack, which was in the RV. It wouldn't have mattered anyway, as his hands were tied tightly behind his back.

Suddenly, Coke remembered that he had one thing in his possession—the Pez dispenser in his back pocket. He struggled to wriggle his right hand around until he could reach it. The Pez dispenser wasn't exactly a knife, but when he flipped the head up, it did have a semi-sharp edge. He began rubbing it against the rope behind his back.

"What are you doing here?" Coke said, just to keep Archie Clone talking while he worked on the rope. "Why are you bothering us again?"

"I already told you," Archie Clone said. "The last living Genius Filer gets a million dollars when they turn twenty-one years old. And I intend to be that last person. Every time one of us dies, it's more money in my pocket. Don't take it personally. You understand, I'm just looking after my long-term financial future."

Archie Clone flipped a switch, and two large glass cylinders slowly lifted up from the floor of the truck where Coke and Pep were sitting, surrounding them. It was like they were sitting inside two enormous test tubes.

"Enough talk," Archie Clone said. "You kids are pretty cool. And you're going to get a lot cooler."

"What is this?" Coke demanded as the glass cylinder reached the level of his neck and locked into place. He was sawing at the rope behind his back with the Pez dispenser but didn't know if it was actually cutting anything.

"Do you kids know what hypothermia is?" Archie Clone asked.

"It's when your body loses heat faster than it can produce it," Coke replied.

"Very good! No wonder you were chosen for The Genius Files," Archie Clone said.

He pulled the handle down on a machine. Soft, yellowish ice cream squeezed out of two tubes hanging from the roof of the truck above the glass cylinders. The ice cream dropped down, splattered against Coke and Pep's heads, and then slid down their faces. Coke stuck out his tongue and tasted it. Vanilla.

"Owwww!" Pep yelled as the ice cream trickled down her back. "That's cold!"

"Very!" Archie Clone said. "But you ain't seen nothin' yet, sister!"

He flipped another switch, and dollops of chocolate ice cream poured down on the twins' heads.

"You're crazy!" Pep shouted.

Archie Clone ignored her.

"You see," he said, "when the human body is

exposed to extreme cold, it can't replenish the heat that's being lost. You get hypothermia. I love the sound of that word. Don't you? Hy-po-ther-mia. Sounds like the name of a Greek god."

Thick globs of chocolate and vanilla ice cream kept squeezing out of spouts over the twins' heads. Ice cream slid down over them and settled to the bottom of the glass cylinders, soaking their sneakers. Coke sawed more frantically on the rope with the Pez dispenser behind his back. The Mister Softee theme jingled repeatedly in the background.

"It's c-c-cold!" Pep muttered.

"Of *course* it's cold," Archie Clone said as frozen treat crept up their ankles. "It's ice cream! I scream. You scream. We all scream for ice cream. *Everybody* likes ice cream, right?"

"I like *eating* it," Coke grunted, "not sitting in it."

"Beggars can't be choosers, Coke," Archie Clone said with a chuckle. "You shouldn't complain about getting too much of a good thing."

"Just take our stupid money!" Pep begged. "We don't care about the million dollars!"

"Yes, it would be so much simpler if we could handle it that way," Archie Clone said. "But rules are rules. Paperwork, and all that nastiness. Legally, you two have to be dead for me to collect my money."

"Help!" Coke shouted, sawing frantically. "Get us out of here."

"You'd be better off conserving your heat energy, Coke," Archie Clone advised. "Nobody can hear you. We're in a tunnel under the park. And nobody would be able to hear you over the Mister Softee jingle anyway. Isn't it delightfully annoying? Maybe next time I'll just play this song in someone's ear over and over again until they kill *themselves*. That would save me a lot of work. Hahahaha!"

The ice cream was getting higher. Coke sneezed.

"Catching a little *cold*, Coke?" Archie Clone asked with fake concern. "You know, normal body temperature is ninety-eight point six degrees. When your temperature drops below ninety-five, you'll get goose bumps and start shivering, first gently, and then violently. Your speech may be slurred. Your limbs may feel numb."

The twins were starting to feel all those symptoms. Ice cream was pouring down on them. It was now almost waist level. Coke wondered if wet rope is easier to cut through, or harder.

"When your temperature drops below ninety-three degrees," Archie Clone continued, "your muscles will become uncoordinated. Your body will start shutting down to preserve glucose. Your blood vessels will contract and your body will use all its remaining energy to keep your vital organs warm. You'll become pale and appear dazed. Your lips, ears, fingers, and toes will turn blue. That's my favorite color! I can't wait!"

"Gee, thanks for the biology lesson," Coke said sarcastically.

"No problem, Coke. I know how much you enjoy learning new things. Well, I think you'll find this bit of trivia interesting. When your body temperature drops below eighty-eight degrees, it will become hard for you to speak. Your pulse and respiration will slow down. Your *brain* will slow down. That famous photographic memory of yours won't work anymore. Your hands won't work anymore either."

The Mister Softee theme droned on. Coke had developed a headache. Archie Clone walked up close to the glass and peered at him.

"You'll become disoriented," he continued. "You'll start behaving irrationally. Your major organs will start to fail. You'll curl up in a fetal position to conserve heat. Finally, your heart will stop. And then you'll die. Ha, ha!"

He had an evil grin on his face. Pep began to cry.

"Oh, don't worry, Pep," Archie Clone said. "This won't take long. That's the nice thing about hypothermia. It's all over before you know it. That is so much more humane than a long, lingering death, don't you think?"

Coke was shivering, and his feet were numb. But Pep was slightly smaller and lighter. She was feeling the effects of the freezing more severely. She could no longer move her fingers.

"Do something!" she told her brother.

Archie Clone pushed the handle back up. The flow of ice cream stopped. Coke and Pep were sitting there, with ice cream up to their necks.

Coke wasn't sure, but he thought he'd made some progress cutting the rope with the Pez dispenser. He would need more time, though.

The only way to get out of the Mister Softee truck alive, he decided, was to keep this nut job talking. Coke would have to reason with him. It hadn't worked with his dad, but it might work with someone whose mind was already twisted.

"I bet you were never one of the cool kids back in school, were you?" Coke asked Archie Clone. "The cool kids picked on you because of your red hair and your weight."

Archie Clone wasn't taking the bait.

"Now *you're* one of the cool kids, aren't you, Coke?" he replied. "Soon you'll be so cool you'll be frozen. Like frozen yogurt."

"What is it with you and food?" Coke asked, shivering.

"First you tried to cook us like french fries, and now you're going to freeze us with ice cream. Maybe you have an eating disorder. Did you ever think of that? You're seriously overweight. Do you wear hats all the time so people won't notice how heavy you are?"

"Oh, do you like this hat?" Archie Clone asked. "It was one of the first ones in my collection."

"You need help, man," Coke said. "I think you may be bipolar."

"Your amateurish attempts at psychology are amusing," Archie Clone told Coke. "You would make a great shrink. That is, if you weren't going to die within the hour."

"Oh, I get it," Coke said, almost smiling. "Food is killing you, so you decided to kill other people by using food. Is that what's going on in that sick mind of yours?"

"Why . . . are you trying to analyze him?" Pep asked her brother. "He's . . . a lunatic!"

But Pep was stuttering and slurring her words, so they could barely be understood. She was shivering violently. Coke didn't have a lot of time. He was still sawing away at the rope behind his back.

"You should listen to your sister," Archie Clone told Coke. "She's a smart cookie. But right now, I'd say her body temperature has dipped to around ninety degrees. Her internal organs are shutting down, and she's sounding like a drunk. I really don't want to see her die."

"So . . . you're . . . going to . . . let me go?" Pep asked hopefully.

"No," Archie Clone replied. "I still want you to die. I just don't want to *see* you die. Death is so . . . morbid. I'm leaving. The authorities can pick up your bodies later."

He pulled off the Mister Softee uniform and went back to the front of the truck.

"Ta-ta, twins," he said as he opened the door. "I'll think of you while I'm spending my million dollars."

"Do something!" Pep yelled when Archie Clone was gone.

"I *am* doing something!"

A few seconds later, the edge of the Pez dispenser finally broke the last strand of the rope around Coke's wrists. He freed his hands and stood up.

"How did you do that?" Pep asked.

"I'll tell you later."

Coke closed his eyes for a moment. He was dizzy, and realized he should not have stood up so quickly.

"Rock the tube!" Pep urged him.

It was a good idea. Coke struggled to put his hands on the top of the circular glass around him. Filled with gallons of ice cream, it was very heavy. But when he put weight on the left side, it moved slightly.

He pushed on the right side, and then back on the

left. It was moving ever so slightly.

"Put all your weight on one side!" Pep yelled.

"It will fall!"

"I know! That's the idea!"

Coke did as his sister suggested. He leaned back and then forward hard. His momentum caused the back edge of the glass tube to lift up and the front to move forward. And then it reached the literal "tipping point." The whole thing toppled over. Shielding his eyes with one hand, Coke fell with it, landing with a crash on the floor. The tube shattered. Ice cream and broken glass were everywhere.

It was no time to do a touchdown dance. Coke jumped up from the dripping mess and grabbed his sister's tube from the top.

"Hold on!" he ordered her.

"To what?"

One good yank and Pep's glass tube toppled over too, with the same result. She was spitting out ice cream. Coke rushed to untie her, and noticed her skin had turned a pale blue. He looked around frantically for something he could use to warm her up.

"Quick!" he shouted, pulling down a handle on one of the machines. "Rub this all over yourself!"

"What is it?"

"Hot fudge," Coke replied as the brown stuff squirted out of the spout.

The hot fudge felt so good on his skin that Coke covered himself with the stuff too. Soon their body temperatures were rising and they were feeling almost normal again. They stepped over the broken glass carefully and ran out of the Mister Softee truck.

If you were at Hershey Park in Hershey, Pennsylvania, and you saw a couple of thirteen-year-old twins covered from head to toe in chocolate sauce, it probably wouldn't seem like such a big deal. But when Coke and Pep staggered out of the tunnel and people saw them stumbling around Cedar Point, there was a lot of pointing, laughing, and cell phone photography.

"Look!" Coke told his sister. "The log flume! Follow me!"

He ran to the shallow pool of water at the end of the log flume ride, and without any hesitation, jumped in. Pep followed.

They splashed around for a minute, and when they climbed out, the ice cream and hot fudge sauce had washed away. They were just two *very* wet kids.

"We better find Mom and Dad," Pep said.

Coke reached for his cell phone and instantly realized it was dead. You can't soak a cell phone in ice cream, hot fudge sauce, and water and expect it to keep working.

In the end, it didn't matter. Dr. and Mrs. McDonald spotted them in the distance.

"What are you going to tell them?" Pep asked her brother.

"The truth," he said, "like I always do."

Their parents rushed over to greet the twins and saw that they were soaking wet.

"What happened to you two?" asked Mrs. McDonald.

"We were kidnapped by an evil Mister Softee," Coke explained. "He tried to induce hypothermia by covering our bodies with ice cream."

"Ha, ha!" Dr. McDonald said. "That's a good one. You kids crack me up."

"Why didn't you call us?" asked their mother. "Why do you think we got you cell phones?"

"They got wet," Coke explained, holding up his useless phone.

"You went for a swim with your cell phone in your pocket?" Mrs. McDonald asked. "Are you out of your minds?"

Dr. McDonald didn't like conflict. He tried to avoid it whenever possible.

"We'll get them new cell phones, honey," he said. "It's no big deal. So, what do you say, how about we get some ice cream?"

"No!"

Chapter 12
DUCT TAPE
AND
ROCK AND
ROLL

Coke and Pep were still in a state of shocked disbelief as the RV pulled out of the huge Cedar Point parking lot. Mya and Bones had told them they would be safe until they got to Washington. And then *this* happened.

Every time they let down their guard, Coke thought, every time they took a deep breath and relaxed a little, something terrible happened. Maybe they would *never* be safe. Maybe these lunatics would be chasing them for the rest of their lives.

"So how were the roller coasters?" Mrs. McDonald

asked excitedly. "Did you have an awesome time?"

"Yeah," Coke replied without enthusiasm. "Awesome."

"Awesome," mumbled Pepsi.

Their parents were disappointed. They had devoted the whole day to doing something just for the kids, but it didn't seem to have made the kids happy. They just sat in the back of the RV, silently. Dr. McDonald figured that after riding a dozen roller coasters and being dropped, flipped, spun, and thrown every which way, maybe the twins' brains were a little out of whack.

It was getting past dinnertime. Dr. McDonald pulled into Cedar Point Camper Village, a few miles away in Sandusky. The campground featured a shuffleboard court, a game room, and an outdoor pool. But all Coke and Pep wanted to do was sleep. They didn't even want dinner. Their parents went to the snack bar to get something for themselves.

Having gone to bed so early, Coke woke up at five a.m., before anyone else in the family. He pulled on a pair of jeans and wandered outside. The campground was quiet. It was peaceful. Nobody else was awake. The only thing open was the game room, so Coke went in.

It was a tiny room, with just three arcade games in it—a shoot-'em-up called Kill Them All, a driving game

called Pedal to the Metal, and an old Ms. Pac-Man machine. Despite the hour, the games were plugged in and turned on, playing their "attract mode." That's the screen display that is shown when nobody is playing an arcade game. The idea is to *attract* the next player. Or, more specifically, the next quarter.

Kill Them All looked interesting. The screen showed guys in camouflage blowing away an army of zombies with machine guns. INSERT COIN flashed in the middle of the screen. Coke stepped up to the console and reached into his pocket. He didn't have any money with him. The coin return was empty. He pushed the start button for the heck of it, on the off chance that the last player had walked away in the middle of a game. Instantly, this flashed on the screen:

EKOC EKOC EKOC EKOC EKOC

Well, it didn't take an encryption expert—or his sister—to figure out that EKOC was COKE backward. And Coke was pretty sure those letters were not referring to the soft drink. In a few seconds they were replaced by this message, in bright blue glowing letters:

WBUAOHYY

It flashed just once and disappeared in a simulated puff of smoke, but Coke had already memorized it. He ran back to the RV and woke up his sister.

"I think we got another cipher," he whispered in her ear.

"Where?" Pep asked, rubbing the sleep from her eyes.

"On the screen of a video game in the game room."

Coke took Pep's notebook and wrote the letters out.

WBUAOHYY

Quietly, so they wouldn't wake their parents, the twins tiptoed outside to sit at the picnic table next to their RV.

"It looks a little like the call letters of a radio station," Pep said as she examined the message.

"Too many letters," Coke told her. "Radio stations

are always WHYY or WCBS, stuff like that."

"You say you saw this on an arcade game screen?" Pep asked. "How do you know it isn't the name of the person who has the high score, or something like that?"

"Before it flashed this message," Coke told her, "it was flashing E-K-O-C over and over again. My name backward. I know it's a message for me."

Pep looked at the letters more closely. Obviously, they didn't mean anything spelled backward. It didn't seem to be an anagram. Every second, third, or fourth letter meant nothing. The consecutive *Y*s made her think "why why" could be part of the message, but nothing else seemed to fit. She tried all the usual codes she knew, but none of them worked. This was a tough one.

The sun was peeking through the trees. People were starting to emerge from their tents and RVs to begin their day.

And suddenly, Pep got it.

"It's simple!" she said excitedly. "This is a half-reversed alphabet!"

Pep took the pen from her brother and wrote out the alphabet in two lines.

ABCDEFGHIJKLM
NOPQRSTUVWXYZ

"I don't get it," Coke said.

Pep drew a line under the cipher: WBUAOHYY.

"If you break the twenty-six letters of the alphabet into two lines of thirteen letters," Pep said, "each letter is directly above or below another letter. The *W* is below the *J*, so the first letter of the message could be *J*."

"If that's true," Coke said, "the second letter of the message would have to be *O*, because *B* is above *O*."

"Right," Pep said. "And the third letter is . . . *H*. And the fourth letter is . . . *N*."

"John!" Coke exclaimed.

So WBUA probably meant JOHN. They continued. *O* was directly below *B*, so the next letter was *B*. *H* was above *U*. *Y* was below *L*. So OHYY meant BULL.

JOHN BULL.

WBUAOHYY meant JOHN BULL.

"You're really good at this, y'know," Coke admitted.

His sister beamed. It wasn't often that she received a compliment from her brother.

"Everybody's good at something," she replied modestly.

"The question becomes," Coke asked, "who is John Bull?"

The door to their RV opened, and Dr. McDonald came out in his pajamas and slippers.

"You two are certainly up early," he said.

Pep hid her notebook behind her back.

"Hey, Dad," said Coke. "Did you ever hear of anybody named John Bull?"

"John Bull?" Dr. McDonald said, searching his memory. "Yeah, but John Bull isn't a person."

"Okay, *what* is John Bull?" Coke asked.

"John Bull is a train," Dr. McDonald replied. "It was one of the first steam locomotives in the world. It was built in the 1830s, I think."

He was right. Dr. McDonald taught American history at San Francisco State University, and it was hard to stump him on anything about the Industrial Revolution. He had written books on the subject.

Coke and Pep glanced at each other, puzzled expressions on their faces. Neither of them could fathom why they would receive a secret message about a train.

"Why do you want to know about John Bull?" their father asked.

"I received a mysterious coded message from a video game in the game room," Coke replied. "It says 'John Bull.'"

"Ha! You kids never cease to amaze me," said Dr. McDonald, shaking his head. Then he went back inside the RV to brush his teeth and get dressed.

Pep turned to the previous page in her notebook and added to her list.

- July 3, two p.m.
- Greensboro lunch counter
- John Bull

Go to Google Maps (http://maps.google.com/).

Click Get Directions.

In the A box, type Sandusky OH.

In the B box, type Avon OH.

Click Get Directions.

"There must be some connection between the Greensboro lunch counter and that train," she said to her brother.

"But what?"

"I guess we'll just have to wait for the next cipher."

"How far are we from Washington now?" Pep asked as they pulled out of the campground and got back on the road.

Mrs. McDonald looked it up on the GPS.

"Four hundred twenty-three miles," she said. "We're getting there."

"So where are we going today?" asked Coke.

"The coolest place in the world," his father said mysteriously.

He slipped a Rolling Stones CD into the slot and drove a little over forty miles, mostly on Route 2 East, following the contour of Lake Erie. And then, quite suddenly, there was a sign that travelers of a certain mind-set find hard to resist:

AVON, OHIO
Duct Tape Capital of the World

"Ben, stop the RV!" Mrs. McDonald shouted. "Pull over!"

The RV screeched to a halt. The refrigerator door flew open, and a jar of Smucker's strawberry jam fell out and hit the floor.

"You gotta be kidding me!" Coke said, throwing up his hands. "*This* is the coolest place in the world? Do we have to go to a museum devoted to *duct tape*?"

As the RV sat on the shoulder of the road, Mrs. McDonald leafed through her Ohio guidebook.

"Relax," she said, when she found the page she was looking for. "They don't have a duct tape museum here. That would be ridiculous."

"Well, that's a relief," Pep said.

"But they have duct tape sculptures," Mrs. McDonald said excitedly, "a duct tape parade, a duct tape fashion show, and a mascot called Duct Tape Duck. Doesn't that sound cool?"

"No," the twins agreed in unison, although, to be completely honest, it did sound pretty cool.

"Kids," Dr. McDonald said, "this is the beauty of traveling cross-country. You never know what you're going to stumble on. This is the adventure. I certainly wouldn't drive two thousand miles to visit the Duct Tape Capital of the World, but here we are. We found it. Something brought us here. It's almost like magic, or fate."

"Duct tape is dumb," Coke said. "I say we get out of here. All in favor, say 'aye.'"

"Aye," said Pep.

"This is not a democracy. We *must* stop here," Mrs. McDonald said with finality. And when Mrs. Bridget McDonald said something with finality, it was final.

They drove all around the small town of Avon looking for duct tape sculptures, with no success. The kids sat in the back, bored.

"Y'know, they say you can solve just about any problem with duct tape," Dr. McDonald said as he leaned forward to read the street signs in the distance.

"Except when the problem is that you're stuck in the Duct Tape Capital of the World," Coke said glumly.

"Is it *duct* tape or *duck* tape?" Mrs. McDonald wondered out loud.

"I believe it's *duct* tape," said Dr. McDonald. "It's mainly used to help seal ducts."

"I think it's *duck* tape, Dad," Pep said. "You use it to help duck seals."

"Duck seals?" asked Mrs. McDonald. "Is that what you get when a duck and a seal mate?"

"No, if a seal is flying in your direction, you need to *duck*," Pep explained. "That's what duck seals means."

"Seals don't fly," Coke pointed out.

"Maybe it's called duck tape because the guy who invented it would throw it at people and they had to duck to avoid being hit by the flying tape," suggested Mrs. McDonald.

"Who cares whether it's duct tape or duck tape?" Coke said, his arms crossed in front of him. "It's *tape*. It's boring. Why are we stopping here?"

The conversation continued along those lines until Dr. McDonald turned onto a street called Just Imagine Drive, where there was an office building with a sign out front.

HENKEL CONSUMER ADHESIVES
Headquarters of Duct Products

"This must be the place!" Mrs. McDonald said, getting out her laptop and camera.

They pulled into the only parking space big enough for an RV and went inside. There was a pretty receptionist sitting behind the front desk.

"May I help you?"

"Yes," Mrs. McDonald said politely. "Can you tell us where is the duct tape parade and what time is the next duct tape fashion show?"

"I'm terribly sorry," the receptionist said, "but none of that is going on today."

"What?!" Mrs. McDonald exclaimed. "We drove all the way from California to see people dressed up in duct tape."

That wasn't exactly true, but it sounded good. Mrs. McDonald was clearly agitated. She put her hands on her hips to demonstrate her annoyance.

"Calm down, Bridge," said Dr. McDonald.

"I *am* calm," Mrs. McDonald said. "But this town advertises itself as the duct tape capital of the world. We've been driving all over town, and I haven't seen any duct tape *anywhere*."

"We have an annual Duct Tape Festival on Father's Day weekend," the receptionist explained. "That's when we crown the Duct Tape Dad of the Year."

"It must be really exciting," Coke said sarcastically.

"I wish to speak to the manager," Mrs. McDonald announced.

"He's at a conference in Denver," said the receptionist as she reached into the drawer next to her.

"They have duct tape conferences?" Coke asked. "Do they actually sit around talking about duct tape?"

The receptionist pulled a small roll of duct tape out of her drawer.

"I'm terribly sorry," she said. "All I can offer you is this complimentary roll of duct tape."

Mrs. McDonald snatched the tape out of her hand and stormed out the door in a huff. The rest of the family followed.

Back in the RV, she flipped the roll of duct tape over her shoulder toward the twins.

"Duck!" she shouted. "Tape!"

Coke played with the roll of duct tape as the RV pulled onto Interstate 90 heading east out of Avon. Dr. McDonald ejected the Rolling Stones and put on a Jimi Hendrix CD, nodding

Go to Google Maps (http://maps.google .com/).

Click Get Directions.

In the A box, type Avon OH.

In the B box, type Cleveland OH.

Click Get Directions.

his head with the music. Mrs. McDonald passed out sandwiches for lunch she had made that morning. After twenty minutes or so on the highway, the tall buildings of a big city came into view in the distance.

"What's that, Dad?" Pep asked.

"Cleveland, Ohio."

"Cleveland?" Coke asked. "Are you taking us to an Indians game?"

"No . . . ," Dr. McDonald replied, and left it at that. He had a little smile on his face.

He got off the road at exit 174B. A sign said CLEVE-LAND MEMORIAL SHOREWAY. The twins tried to figure out where they were going as they passed by a little airport near the Lake Erie waterfront.

Soon, a few blocks ahead, Pep spotted a large glass building that was shaped like a pyramid.

"What's that?" Pep asked.

"Only the coolest place in the world," Dr. McDonald replied.

As they got closer, a sign came into view.

"All right!" both kids shouted.

The twins were surprised that their father, a serious student of American history, would get excited about a museum devoted to rock music. But Dr. McDonald explained to them that rock and roll is more than just a style of music. It changed the way we live, the way we dress, how we are entertained, and our attitudes on so many issues.

He pulled the RV into the parking lot and climbed out with a spring in his step, whistling "I Love Rock 'n' Roll" by Joan Jett and the Blackhearts. Everybody was excited. Mrs. McDonald brought along her camera and notepad. Coke threw the roll of duct tape into his backpack and slung it over his shoulder. Pep didn't bring anything. She hopped out of the RV and began to sing as she skipped across the parking lot.

"*Hit me with your pet shark! Come on and hit me with your pet shark. . . .*"

"Wait a minute," Coke interrupted his sister. "What did you just say?"

"I said 'hit me with your pet shark.'"

"It's not 'hit me with your pet shark,' you dope!" Coke told her. "It's 'hit me with your *best shot.*'"

"It is not!" Pep said defensively.

"It is too!"

"Mom?"

"I'm afraid your brother is right, honey," Mrs. McDonald told Pep. "It's 'hit me with your best shot.' I remember that song. It was by Pat Benatar."

Pep, who had gone through her entire thirteen years thinking the song went 'hit me with your pet shark,' had never been so humiliated. She broke down in tears. Coke couldn't help but laugh, but both parents came to Pep's side.

"Don't feel bad, sweetie," Dr. McDonald said as he put his arm around Pep. "People misinterpret song lyrics all the time. When I was a kid, there was a song called 'When a Man Loves a Woman' by Percy Sledge. I always thought he was singing 'When a Man Loves a Walnut.'"

"Really?" Pep said, crying and laughing at the same time.

"You know that song 'Blowin' in the Wind' by Bob Dylan?" asked Mrs. McDonald. "When I was a kid, I thought he was singing, 'the ants are my friends, blowin' in the wind.'"

"You made that up!" Pep said, wiping her eyes.

"I didn't, really!" her mother said. "I *still* think that's what it sounds like."

"Come to think of it," Coke said, trying to cheer up his sister, "'hit me with your pet shark' is *better* than 'hit me with your best shot.'"

Pep snapped out of it, and the family entered the huge building in a good mood. Dr. McDonald bought tickets and looked over the map of the museum. There were seven floors connected by escalators, with five little theaters showing videos.

Everyone had his or her own interests. The grown-ups wanted to see the exhibits devoted to blues, country, and rockabilly music. The kids wanted to head straight for rap, punk, and hip-hop. Pep had become a Beatles freak after playing Rock Band with her friends back home. Coke preferred heavy metal. Mrs. McDonald wanted to learn about Jimi Hendrix. Dr. McDonald was more interested in Les Paul and the invention of the electric guitar. There was so much *stuff*. It would take up most of the afternoon to see the whole place.

Rather than walking the museum as a foursome, everyone agreed they could cover more ground in a shorter period of time if they split up.

"The museum closes at five thirty," Mrs. McDonald told the twins. "Meet you at the bench out front at that time. Don't be late!"

The kids took off in one direction, and the parents went in another one.

"Do you think we'll be safe in here?" Pep asked her brother. "Every time we go off without Mom and Dad, something happens."

"What could possibly happen in here?" Coke replied. "You're being paranoid."

There are lots of cool places mentioned in this book, but the Rock and Roll Hall of Fame is probably the coolest. If you love music, you should definitely go there at some point in your life.

The twins jumped from exhibit to exhibit, sometimes looking at every object very closely and other times skipping them entirely. The museum is filled with photos, posters, videos, handwritten lyrics to songs, stage costumes, and guitars and cars of the stars. You can put on headphones and listen to just about every rock song ever recorded.

"Look, there's Jim Morrison's Cub Scout uniform," Coke pointed out.

"Who's Jim Morrison?" Pep asked.

"Some guy who died."

There are no statues or plaques of the musicians who have been inducted into the Rock and Roll Hall of Fame. Instead, there's a long, curving wall with all their signatures.

By five o'clock Coke and Pep had been through most of the exhibits, taking the escalators higher and higher until they had reached the top floor.

"We should probably head back down," Pep said. "Mom and Dad told us to meet them on the bench out front at five thirty."

"Relax," Coke told his sister. "Hey, check this out."

There was a door off to one side, where most people would not see it. The word RECORDING was above the door, and next to the letters was a little red light-bulb that was lit up.

"It's a studio," Pep said. "They probably record music or commercials in there."

"Let's go in," Coke said.

"We're not allowed in there," said Pep.

"Says who?" Coke replied. "I don't see any 'Do Not Enter' sign. It's a museum. It's open to the public. We paid our admission. Come on."

He pulled open the door. Reluctantly, Pep followed. They were in a tiny room now, not much bigger than an old-fashioned telephone booth. There was another door on the other side. The first door clicked shut behind them.

"I don't like this," Pep said nervously.

"Shhhhh," her brother said.

He pushed on the other door, and it opened into a larger room dominated by a huge control panel with hundreds of dials, knobs, and switches on it. Neither of the twins had ever been in a recording studio before. It almost looked like the cockpit of a plane.

There were three large chairs in front of the control panel. All of them swiveled around, as if on cue.

There were three people sitting in the chairs—the two bowler dudes and Mrs. Higgins.

Chapter 13
THE LOUD FAMILY

"Eeeekkk!" Pep screamed. "It's them!"

Coke turned to grab for the door handle. It was locked. They were trapped. Again.

"Well . . . well . . . well," said Mrs. Higgins.

The bowler dudes smiled and laughed their stupid laughs. Each of them had a club, like the kind policemen carry. They hit the clubs rhythmically into the palm of one hand.

"How did you get in here?" Pep demanded.

"The question isn't how we got in here," Mrs. Higgins replied. "The question is how are *you* going to get *out*?"

"Good one, Mrs. H.," the mustachioed bowler dude said, chuckling.

Coke looked around quickly. They were at the very top of the pyramid-shaped building. He could see the Lake Erie waterfront and the sky through the glass windows surrounding them on all sides. The only exit was locked. They were outnumbered. He had no weapons, while both of the bowler dudes had clubs. There was an electric guitar sitting in a stand on the floor. But what was he going to do, hit somebody over the head with it? It was a bad situation.

Pep couldn't help but marvel at Mrs. Higgins. One day she was working as a paid assassin for Dr. Warsaw. The next day she managed to get a job working in the public relations department of the Chicago Cubs. And now she had somehow talked her way into the Rock and Roll Hall of Fame. Maybe she was right—she *did* have good people skills.

"That wasn't very nice what you kids did at Wrigley Field," Mrs. Higgins said, wagging a finger at them. "The fans were very upset that the Cubs forfeited the game."

"It was *your* fault!" Pep shouted. "You told us there was a bomb in the dugout! You gave us those T-shirts! You almost got us killed!"

"I'll try harder this time."

"Good one, Mrs. H.," said the clean-shaven bowler dude.

Both bowler dudes laughed and slapped the clubs into their palms. There would be no way to overpower them.

"What are you going to do now," Coke asked, "blow up the Rock and Roll Hall of Fame?"

"Heavens no!" Mrs. Higgins replied. "I *love* rock and roll. Put another dime in the jukebox, baby!"

One of the bowler dudes flipped a switch on the control panel, and heavy metal music filled the studio.

"Ah, Megadeth," Mrs. Higgins said. "My favorite slash metal band. And I can really relate to this album—*Killing Is My Business . . . and Business Is Good*."

The bowler dudes chuckled.

"Good one, Mrs. H.," they both said.

"Stop saying that!" Mrs. Higgins scolded them. "It's annoying."

"Yes, Mrs. H."

"You kids like loud rock music, don't you?" she asked sweetly. "I'll just turn this up a little."

She turned a dial on the control panel, and the music got louder. Both bowler dudes took earplugs out of their pockets and stuck them in their ears.

"You're smart kids," Mrs. Higgins continued. "I'm sure you know that sound travels in waves through the air. You can't see them, but you can feel the vibrations."

"We don't need your boring science lesson," Coke spat.

"You're right, Coke," she agreed. "I don't want to bore you. I want to *kill* you."

"Good one—"

"Shut up!" Mrs. Higgins hollered at the bowler dude, causing him to stop talking instantly.

"I *told* you we shouldn't have come in here!" Pep said to her brother, tears running down her face. "You should listen to me for a change!"

"Don't bicker, kids," Mrs. Higgins said. "It will all be over soon."

She turned the dial again, and the music got louder.

"The human ear is a marvelous organ, isn't it?" Mrs. Higgins said. "Sound waves enter the outer ear like a funnel, and they shoot through the ear canal to vibrate the eardrum."

"We don't care what you have to say!" Pep yelled. But Mrs. Higgins kept right on going.

"There are three tiny bones in your middle ear, and they intensify the vibrations and deliver them to the inner ear. That's where the cochlea is. It looks like a little clamshell, and it's filled with fluid. The sound waves make the fluid move. There are thousands of tiny hairlike cells in there that connect to the acoustic nerve, which sends electro-chemical signals to the brain. And that's how you hear things. Isn't that interesting?"

"No!" Coke shouted over the music.

"Oh, I'm terribly sorry," Mrs. Higgins said. "I was boring you again, wasn't I?"

She turned the dial, and the volume went up some more. The music had became uncomfortably loud.

"Turn it down," Pep said, putting her hands over her ears.

"Did you say turn it up?" asked Mrs. Higgins, giving the dial another twist. "Sure."

"No, I said turn it *down*!"

"Can't hear you," shouted Mrs. Higgins. "It's quite noisy in here."

"Turn it *down*!" Coke screamed.

Mrs. Higgins turned the dial the other way, and the volume went down so low that the music could barely be heard. The twins took their hands off their ears.

"But Coke," Mrs. Higgins said, "I thought you *liked* your music loud."

"Not *that* loud," he replied.

"You know all about decibel levels, right?" Mrs.

Higgins asked. "The sound of human breathing is about ten decibels."

She turned up the volume on the control panel slightly. Megadeth's "The Skull Beneath the Skin" was playing.

"Normal speech is sixty decibels."

She turned the volume up a little more.

"A vacuum cleaner is eighty decibels."

She twisted the dial again and put on a set of noise-canceling headphones over her ears.

"A motorcycle is a hundred and five."

Twist.

The twins put their hands over their ears again. Pep was getting a headache. Mrs. Higgins leaned toward them, her eyes flashing.

"Pain begins at a hundred twenty decibels," she shouted over "The Skull Beneath the Skin." "A jet taking off is a hundred forty. At one hundred fifty, your chest wall starts vibrating. At one hundred sixty, the thin membrane of your eardrum is shredded instantly. At one hundred eighty, your hearing tissue dies. The small bones in your ear snap, like twigs. And you know how glass will shatter at very high frequencies? Any sound louder than one hundred eighty decibels will literally make your heads explode!"

"I love a happy ending!" yelled the clean-shaven bowler dude.

"They've got some really powerful speakers in this studio," hollered Mrs. Higgins over the music. "They can pump out more than two hundred decibels of sound. Of course, nobody would ever turn them up that high. It would be . . . *dangerous*."

"You're crazy!" Pep yelled, holding her hands tightly over her ears. "Let us out!"

"Get this on tape, boys," Mrs. Higgins shouted. "I want to record the sound of their heads exploding, so I can play it over and over again to cheer me up when I'm in a bad mood. This is what they get for killing my boyfriend."

The mustachioed bowler dude pushed a button on the control panel. Mrs. Higgins cranked up the volume one more time.

"Turn it off!" Coke begged. "Please, turn it off!"

Instead of turning it off, Mrs. Higgins yanked the dial right out of the control panel. There would be no way to turn it left or right. The volume was locked into place.

"I hate to be a party pooper, but we should go," Mrs. Higgins said, getting up from her chair. "It's way too noisy in here."

She went to the door and opened it with a key.

The bowler dudes followed her out, pushing the kids away so they couldn't do the same. Just before the door closed, Mrs. Higgins poked her head back inside for a moment.

"To paraphrase the Who," she said, "I hope you die before you get old."

The door closed with a sharp click.

Coke and Pep looked at each other helplessly. Then they turned around and pounced on the control panel, turning every dial and flipping every switch in the hope that one of them would turn down the music.

Nothing worked.

Coke looked around. If he could destroy the speaker, the sound would stop. But the speaker was behind a thick metal screen.

And then he got an idea. He reached into his backpack and pulled out his roll of duct tape. He handed it to Pep.

"What do you want me to do with *that*?" she shouted over the music.

"Wrap it around my head!" he shouted back. "Cover my ears!"

She did what he said, pulling the tape around and around her brother's head, trying to avoid covering his eyes. Then he took the roll of tape and did the same to her. They looked like a couple of mummies, but the sound reaching their ears was significantly reduced.

Duct tape truly *is* the solution to just about any problem.

"We gotta get out of this place," Coke shouted to his sister, "if it's the last thing we ever do!"

"What?" Pep asked, unable to hear a thing.

"Never mind," Coke said, grabbing the electric guitar on the floor. He climbed up on the control panel and tapped the neck of the guitar against the glass ceiling of the studio.

"What are you doing?" Pep screamed. "Don't break the glass! We'll get in trouble!"

"What?" Coke asked. He hadn't heard a word she said.

He took the guitar again, and this time rammed the neck *hard* against a panel of the glass. It shattered, falling inside the studio and nearly hitting Coke on the way down. He rubbed the guitar against the remaining shards of glass to knock them out and make the opening a little larger.

"Oh, and I suppose you're going to climb up there and slide down outside of the pyramid," Pep shouted. "You're crazy!"

"What?"

"Forget it."

Coke put the guitar back in its stand and climbed up on the control panel again. Then he reached up and pulled himself through the hole he had made, grabbing onto the frame around the window. He was on top of the Rock and Roll Hall of Fame. He reached his hand down to help Pep climb up there with him.

"I can't do it!" she screamed, shaking her head.

"Come on!"

She stepped up on the control panel tentatively, reached up, and took her brother's hand. He gripped it tightly and nodded his head to encourage her.

"You can do this, Pep," he said.

"What?"

He pulled her up and she held on for dear life. She managed to get her legs up on the window frame and squeeze through the opening. She was outside. She looked around to see the Cleveland skyline on one side and Lake Erie on the other. They were so high. The music was no longer blasting at their ears.

"Okay, let's go!" Coke said. "We'll slide down together!"

"No way."

"Come on," Coke said, "just like we used to do it on the slide at the playground when we were little."

She crawled over his leg so she could sit in front of

him, with his arms and legs wrapped around her.

"I'm scared," she said.

"Hold on," Coke replied. "Close your eyes."

She did, and he pushed off. They began to slide down the pyramid, slowly at first. When it seemed like they were picking up too much speed, Coke pressed the bottoms of his sneakers against the glass to slow them down. When he felt in control again, he eased up on the "brakes" and let them just slide.

"Woo-hoo!" Coke hollered. "This is better than the roller coasters at Cedar Point!"

When they were halfway down, Pep finally opened her eyes. Looking below, she could see her parents sitting on the bench where they had agreed to meet at five thirty. The twins were heading directly toward them.

Down on the bench, Mrs. McDonald looked at her watch.

"The kids are late," she said.

"We specifically told them to be here at five thirty," said Dr. McDonald.

"Kids," they both muttered.

Toward the bottom of the pyramid, Pep closed her eyes again.

"We're going to land on Mom and Dad!" she screamed.

Luckily, they didn't. They landed in some thick bushes right *behind* their parents. The bushes served to cushion the impact.

"Ooooooooooof!"

After hearing two thuds in the bushes behind them, Dr. and Mrs. McDonald turned around. Coke and Pep stood up and brushed themselves off.

"When did you kids get here?" Dr. McDonald said. "We didn't even see you come out the door."

"We didn't," Coke said honestly. "We slid down the outside."

"Very funny," Mrs. McDonald said. "Why do you have duct tape wrapped around your heads?"

"Huh?" Coke said. "Can't hear you, Mom. I have duct tape wrapped around my head."

Mrs. McDonald carefully removed the duct tape from Coke, trying her best not to rip out his hair.

"I asked you why you have duct tape wrapped around your head," she said.

"Oh, this," Coke replied. "Remember Mrs. Higgins, the health teacher at school? Well, she locked us in a recording studio at the top of the Hall of Fame and played Megadeth at full blast. So we wrapped duct tape around our ears to reduce the noise level so our heads wouldn't explode."

Dr. McDonald chuckled appreciatively.

"Hahaha!" he said. "That's a good one."

Behind their parents' backs, Coke and Pep shook their heads. The McDonalds walked back to the RV in the parking lot. Coke checked his arms and legs to see if he had any scratches or bruises.

"Tell me the truth," Dr. McDonald said as they put their seat belts on. "What's the deal with the duct tape?"

"The truth?" Coke asked.

"Yeah."

"It's the latest thing, Dad," Coke explained. "Didn't you read about it in the paper? You wrap duct tape around your head. It's a fashion statement. All the kids are doing it."

"At least they didn't get tattoos, dear," said Mrs. McDonald.

"Can we get out of here?" Pep asked. "I've had enough of duct tape and rock and roll for the day."

Chapter 14

PRESERVING THE HOOVER LEGACY

Dr. McDonald pulled out of the Rock and Roll Hall of Fame parking lot and drove past the stadium where the Cleveland Indians play their home games.

"I'm *so* disappointed," Mrs. McDonald said as she thumbed through her Ohio guidebook.

"What's wrong, honey?"

"The Goodyear World of Rubber Museum is closed," she said sadly. "It would have been perfect for *Amazing but True*."

"What a shame," Dr. McDonald said, rolling his eyes. "I'm so sorry."

On the inside, he was cheering. The *last* thing he wanted to do was visit a museum devoted to rubber. This would be one less ridiculous tourist attraction that he would have to endure.

"But I was thinking that we could visit the Goodyear Airdock," Mrs. McDonald said. "It's in Akron, less than an hour south of here."

"Airdock? What's that?" Dr. McDonald asked, suspiciously.

"It's a place where they used to build Goodyear blimps," she told him. "It's twenty-two stories high, and four football fields could fit inside at the same time. It says here it's the largest building in the world that doesn't have interior supports. It's so big that sometimes it even *rains* inside!"

"Wow," Dr. McDonald said.

He turned around to see the twins' reaction. They just stared back, expressionless.

"What do you think, kids?" he asked. "Would it be fun to visit the largest building in the world?"

"Whatever."

The twins weren't listening. Pep was feeling guilty about breaking the window at the top of the Rock and Roll Hall of Fame. If anybody found out who did it, they could get into serious trouble. And Coke was thinking about Mrs. Higgins. She had tried to kill them three, four, maybe *five* times now. Each time, they escaped. She must be *really* mad, and determined. What would she try next? When he tried not to think about it, the image of Archie Clone popped into his head. *That* lunatic was running around free somewhere, too.

Cleveland is only about 370 miles from Washington. If they drove straight through the night, it would be possible to get there in seven hours. But everyone was tired and hungry.

The closer they got to their final destination, the more nervous Coke and Pep became. Something evil was waiting for them there. They knew that much. They didn't know what it was, or what it would do. But they knew it was out there, tracking their every move.

Dr. McDonald pulled onto Interstate 71 heading south and got off at exit 226. It wasn't long until they had reached Willow Lake Park, a campground in Brunswick, Ohio. It was a nice place, with horseshoe pits, miniature golf, and a basketball court. The family worked together to make a quick dinner, did a dump of the RV's septic tank, threw a few horseshoes, and called it a day.

"I have an announcement to make," Dr. McDonald said over breakfast the next morning. "I've been thinking about this for a long time, and I've decided on the subject for my next book."

"What is it, dear?" asked Mrs. McDonald as she leafed through her Ohio guidebook.

"I'm going to write a biography," Dr. McDonald replied, "of Herbert Hoover."

"You should write about one of the more famous presidents, Dad," Coke said. "Like Washington, or Lincoln, or Kennedy. That would sell lots more books."

"Yeah, why him, Dad?" asked Pep. "Wasn't Hoover the president who got us into the Depression?"

"You see? That's all anyone knows about Hoover," Dr. McDonald said. "But he was a fascinating man. Did you know that he never took any money for being president of the United States? He donated his salary to charity."

"Is that so?" asked Mrs. McDonald, looking up from her book.

"I'll bet you didn't know that President Hoover spoke Chinese," Dr. McDonald continued, "and his vice president, Charles Curtis, was part Native American."

"I actually knew that," Coke said.

"But did you know that Hoover was the first president to have a telephone on his desk? Did you know that his son had a pet alligator? I'll bet you didn't know that President Hoover wouldn't let his wife see the White House servants. It's true. Whenever she walked into a room, they had to go hide in a closet."

"President Hoover sounds like a weirdo, Dad," Coke remarked.

"Exactly!" Dr. McDonald said. "People *love* weirdos. They'll want to know more about him."

"I think it's a great idea, Dad," Pep said enthusiastically. "I say go for it."

At that point, Mrs. McDonald let out a gasp.

"I can't believe it!" she exclaimed.

"What?"

"This is an amazing coincidence," she said. "It says here that the Hoover Historical Center is in North Canton, Ohio. That's less than an hour from here! And it's even in the right direction."

"Let's go!" Dr. McDonald shouted.

Even the kids felt good about going to the Hoover Historical Center. Dr. McDonald had sacrificed so much on the trip for the rest of the family. They knew their father didn't enjoy going to silly museums and tacky tourist sites. But he went along with the rest of the family and was always a good sport. The family hadn't gone

Go to Google Maps (http://maps.google.com/).

Click Get Directions.

In the A box, type Brunswick OH.

In the B box, type North Canton OH.

Click Get Directions.

anywhere just for *him* since their short trip to the Bonneville Salt Flats, way back in Utah.

Dr. McDonald drove back on Route 71 South and went seven miles. Then he cut across to Route 77 South to North Canton.

Coke knew that the Pro Football Hall of Fame was right nearby, in Canton, Ohio. It would be much more fun for him to go there. But he was the only football fan in the family, and it would be so much more important for his dad to gather some information for his book on President Hoover. Besides, *everybody* goes to the Football Hall of Fame. How many people can say they've been to the Hoover Historical Center?

"I'm thinking of calling my book *Hoover: The Forgotten President*," Dr. McDonald said as he drove. "What do you think?"

"I like that," Mrs. McDonald said as she plugged the address of the Hoover Historical Center into the GPS. It led them to the campus of Walsh University.

"*You have reached your destination*," the voice on the GPS announced.

The RV stopped in front of an old white farmhouse with red, white, and blue bunting over the porch and an American flag on the front lawn. A white picket fence surrounded the house. It looked very "American."

"I wonder if this was President Hoover's boyhood home," Mrs. McDonald said.

"Hmmm, I thought he grew up in Iowa," said Dr. McDonald.

He pulled out a pen and paper so he could take notes. Mrs. McDonald volunteered to take photos that could be used in the book. Coke and Pep prepared themselves mentally for a few hours of boredom. Even if President Hoover *did* get his son a pet alligator, this place was probably going to be—as Coke put it—"Snoozeville."

They opened the gate and went inside the Hoover Historical Center. An older woman was sitting behind a desk. A sign behind her said PRESERVING THE HOOVER LEGACY. The admission was five dollars.

"Excuse me," Dr. McDonald said. "I'm a professor at San Francisco State University, and I'm going to be writing a book about President Hoover. Would I be able to look at his personal papers?"

The woman stared at him for a moment, then asked him to repeat his request. He did.

"I'm terribly sorry, sir," she said. "We don't have anything about President Hoover here."

"I beg your pardon?" Dr. McDonald said. "This is the Hoover Historical Center. Certainly you must have a *lot* of information about Herbert Hoover."

"There must be some mistake, sir," she replied. "This is a *vacuum cleaner museum*."

"What?!"

"The Hoover Historical Center is about the history of the Hoover Vacuum Cleaner Company," she informed him. "It's not about Herbert Hoover."

"You're kidding me, right?" Dr. McDonald said, his voice rising slightly. He looked around to see if there might be a camera crew hiding somewhere to film his reaction for one of those TV shows where they pull pranks on people.

"The Hoover Historical Center is the boyhood home of William H. Hoover," she informed him. "It's about vacuum cleaners. Would you like a guided tour?"

Dr. McDonald's eyes were bulging out of his head.

"The vacuum is between your ears!" Dr. McDonald thundered at the woman. "I didn't drive two thousand miles to go to a museum about vacuum cleaners!"

"Calm down, honey," Mrs. McDonald said.

"I'm really sorry," said the receptionist. "But I think you'll find our exhibits to be quite interesting."

In fact, the Hoover Historical Center *was* quite interesting, after the rest of the family managed to calm Dr. McDonald down and agree to take the tour.

It turns out that in 1907 a janitor named Murray Spangler invented a primitive vacuum cleaner because his asthma flared up whenever he swept the floor with a broom. He rigged up a simple machine using a soap box, a fan, a pillowcase, and a broom handle and called the device a "suction sweeper." William H. "Boss" Hoover was a wealthy businessman who bought Spangler out and started the company.

"This is perfect for *Amazing but True*!" Mrs. McDonald kept saying as she snapped pictures. "My readers will love this!"

The history of Hoover was called (naturally) "Sweeping Changes." Display cases were filled with antique vacuums, old ads, and even a recording of Hoover salesmen singing the company theme song from the 1920s—"All the Dirt, All the Grit."

"I wish I had that song on my iPod," Coke remarked.

"This is like the history of *dirt*," noted Pep with a giggle.

"I had no idea that disposable vacuum cleaner bags could be so interesting," said Mrs. McDonald. "And who knew that Hoover came up with the vacuum cleaner headlight?"

The family spent over an hour in the museum, until they felt that they knew just about everything there was to know about vacuum cleaners.

"That *was* fascinating," Dr. McDonald admitted as they piled back into the RV. "Maybe instead of writing about President Hoover, I should write a book about the history of vacuum cleaners."

"That book would really suck, Dad," Coke remarked.

Chapter 15

THE NEXT CIPHER

When the McDonald family climbed back into the RV after the vacuum cleaner episode, there was a six-by-nine-inch manila envelope on Coke's seat. He didn't think anything of it at first and put it aside. It wasn't until a few minutes later that he realized the envelope had not been there before. He tore it open. Inside was a sheet of lined paper with this written on it:

SSGBETPLARAAENXRNDNX

Another cipher.

"Oh no," Coke muttered out loud.

"What is it, honey?" asked his mother from the front of the RV.

"Nothing, Mom," Coke said. "I just . . . dropped something."

Silently, he handed Pep the sheet of paper. His photographic memory was very powerful, but when it came to deciphering secret messages, he was pretty much useless.

Pep looked over the paper. There were no obvious patterns. Backward, the letters meant nothing. Skipping letters didn't work. None of the usual strategies she knew seemed to fit. Embedded words—like BET—were always a distraction.

She could solve some ciphers almost instantly. This one was not easy. It would take some time.

Dr. McDonald suddenly pulled off the road into a strip mall.

"Why are we stopping, Ben?" asked Mrs. McDonald.

"I saw a cell phone store," he replied. "We need to get new ones for the kids."

"Oh yeah . . ."

You, dear reader, who has been

Go to Google Maps (http://maps.google.com/).

Click Get Directions.

In the A box, type North Canton OH.

In the B box, type Somerset PA.

Click Get Directions.

paying careful attention and perhaps even taking notes, certainly recall that Coke's and Pep's cell phones were ruined—they had been soaked in ice cream, hot chocolate sauce, and water back at the amusement park in Sandusky. While the twins didn't really *need* to have cell phones, Dr. McDonald considered it a safety issue. If for some reason the family got separated, they would be able to get in touch with one another if they all had cell phones.

After they picked out phones, Coke and Pep ducked outside the store while their parents worked out the details with a clerk.

"Did you figure out the cipher yet?" Coke asked his sister.

"You just gave it to me, like, a *minute* ago!" she replied, annoyed.

"Do you think you'll be able to figure it out?"

"I don't know," Pep said irritably. "I'll do my best."

Coke paced nervously back and forth outside the store, worried that they were getting closer to Washington.

"Where are Mya and Bones?" he asked. "They were supposed to help us, protect us. Some help they are. When was the last time we saw them? In that motel? We'll probably never see them again. They abandoned us."

"Look, they said they'd meet us in Washington," Pep told her brother. "I believe them."

"Yeah, they also said we could relax and have fun until we got to Washington," Coke said bitterly. "But Archie Clone almost killed us at the amusement park, and Mrs. Higgins almost killed us at the Rock and Roll Hall of Fame. Maybe they're working together. Mya and Bones were nowhere in sight. And now we're getting all these ciphers that make no sense at all."

"You need to calm down," Pep said. "We're going to need you to be sharp when we get to D.C."

She was right, and Coke knew it. Usually it was Pep who was the nervous one. But the closer they got to Washington, the more anxious Coke had become. He reminded himself to stay strong, stay focused. One slip and it could be all over for both of them.

"Okay!" Mrs. McDonald said as she came out of the cell phone store and handed the twins their new phones. "You kids need to be careful with these. We don't want to replace them again."

"Now let's put some miles away today," Dr. McDonald said. "Washington, here we come!"

Soon they were cruising at seventy miles per hour down Interstate 76, a superhighway that starts near Akron, Ohio, and goes all the way to New Jersey. They had been in the state of Ohio for a long time. But soon this sign appeared at the side of the road:

"Woo-hoo!" Coke shouted. "The Keystone State! We can get some keystones here."

"What's a keystone?" asked Pep.

"I have no idea," Coke said. "But I do know that Pennsylvania is a state of firsts. They had the first hospital in America. The first library and zoo. They had the first newspaper, the first TV and radio broadcasts. Pennsylvania had the first capital of the United States. And most importantly, the banana split was invented here!"

"You are such a wealth of totally useless information," Pep said.

"You wish you were me," her brother replied.

Dr. McDonald pushed his foot down on the accelerator just a little bit harder. The speedometer nudged past seventy, well above the speed limit. He hoped he wouldn't get a ticket.

All four McDonalds looked out the window. After they had crossed the Pennsylvania state line, there was the definite feeling that they had finally reached the eastern part of the country. They were just 287 miles from Washington now. It no longer felt like a distant land.

Two weeks earlier, Coke and Pep had been on the beach of the Pacific Ocean. Now, the Atlantic Ocean was just a few hours away. Soon they would be in the nation's capital. As they looked out the window and watched the world go by, they wondered what awaited them in Washington.

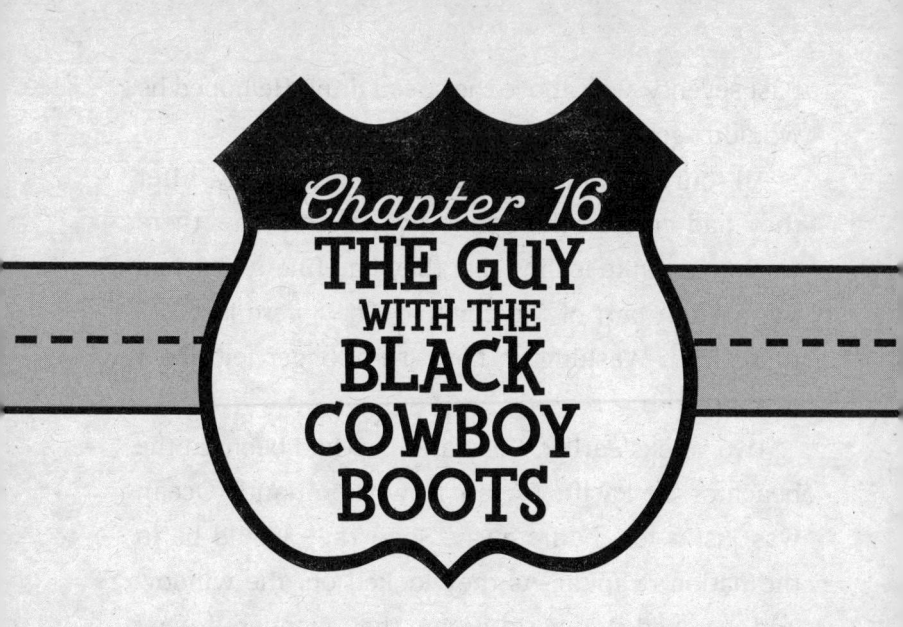

Chapter 16
THE GUY
WITH THE
BLACK
COWBOY
BOOTS

"**H**ey guys, guess what?" Mrs. McDonald said excitedly. "It says here that there's a flying saucer parked in a field in Mars, Pennsylvania."

"No!" shouted Dr. McDonald. "We're not going!"

He had nothing against flying saucers or visiting the town of Mars, Pennsylvania. But Dr. McDonald was anxious to get to Washington. He had never been to the National Air and Space Museum. The World War II Memorial had not been built the last time he was in the nation's capital. The McDonalds weren't planning to spend a lot of days in Washington, and one of them would be taken up by his sister-in-law's wedding. So he didn't want to waste time looking at flying saucers in Pennsylvania.

Mrs. McDonald continued to leaf through her guidebook.

"There's a zombie museum near Pittsburgh," she noted. "It's in the mall where they shot the movie *Dawn of the Dead*."

"No!" said Dr. McDonald.

"We could visit Mister Ed's Elephant Museum in Orrtanna," she said. "It has over six thousand—"

"No!"

"In North Huntingdon, there's a McDonald's that has a fourteen-foot-tall Big Mac—"

"No!"

"They have a Big Mac Sauce Gun—"

"No!"

"There's this place called the House of Oddities near Pittsburgh—"

"No!"

"It's only a few miles out of our way—"

"No!"

Dr. McDonald had been pretty flexible and understanding up until this point. He had agreed to stop at just about every ridiculous tourist trap as they made their way cross-country. They had visited museums devoted to Pez, yo-yos, mustard, and cannibals. They had visited the largest ball of twine in the world. They had even visited the *second* largest ball of twine in the world. But now he felt the need to assert himself—especially after the Hoover Historical Center turned out to be about the vacuum cleaner instead of the president. So he drove on.

In Pennsylvania, Interstate 76 is called the Pennsylvania Turnpike. It extends 359 miles across the state. Some people call it the "Tunnel Highway" because it goes through a number of tunnels that were blasted in the mountains.

There was little traffic on the turnpike, and they were making good time. But eventually driver fatigue set in and Dr. McDonald pulled off I-76 near Somerset, Pennsylvania. It was just a few miles to Pioneer Park Campground, at the foot of the Laurel Ridge Mountains.

After a quick dinner, the family went their separate ways for a while. Dr. McDonald bought a newspaper and found an empty hammock where he could read. Mrs. McDonald updated the *Amazing but True* website. Coke went to check out the lake, where some kids were fishing. Pep worked on the latest cipher they had received, with no success.

The McDonalds had enjoyed a lot of togetherness

over the last two weeks, and everybody was starting to feel the need for a little alone time. As darkness fell, they all returned to the RV to go to bed.

In the middle of the night, Coke began talking in his sleep.

"Don't wanna go to Washington," he grunted, almost incoherently. "Mrs. Higgins . . . bowler dudes . . . Archie Clone . . . Don't wanna go . . . Wanna go home . . ."

Eventually, the noise woke up his parents. They climbed out of bed to make sure Coke was okay.

"Don't wanna go . . . D.C. . . . Don't wanna go . . . Wanna go home . . ."

"He's having a nightmare," Dr. McDonald whispered.

"I guess he *really* doesn't want to go to my sister's wedding," Mrs. McDonald whispered back.

"Boys hate getting dressed up," said Dr. McDonald. "I'll bet that's it. When I was a kid, I'd do anything to get out of wearing a jacket and tie."

"Shhhh," Mrs. McDonald whispered as she tucked the covers in around Coke. "Everything will be fine, honey."

In the morning, they were back on the turnpike by nine o'clock. Pep looked at her new cell phone and announced that it was the first of July. Three days until the big wedding. Two days until . . . *something* was going to happen in Washington. She had no idea what it was going to be.

He had driven about thirty miles when Dr. McDonald noticed the needle on the gas gauge was only slightly above *E.* At the next rest area—in Bedford, Pennsylvania—he pulled into the gas station to fill up the tank.

While his father took care of the gas and his sister went to buy a pack of gum, Coke went off to use the restroom.

"What's wrong with the bathroom in the RV?" his mother asked.

"It's gross, Mom."

Coke pulled open the door to the men's bathroom and looked around, just to be on the safe side. Nobody was in there. The three stalls were empty, and Coke went into the middle one.

While he was in there doing his business, he heard the door open and footsteps enter the men's restroom. Somebody was whistling "The Yellow Rose of Texas." Coke leaned forward and peeked under the stall door to see that the guy who came in was wearing black cowboy boots. Peeking through the narrow crack near the stall door, Coke could see the guy was wearing a large cowboy hat. But he couldn't see the guy's face. There was the sound of water in a sink, and then the electric hand dryer.

The guy was standing just a foot or two away from the stall. It made Coke feel uncomfortable, and he didn't stand up even though he was finished. He didn't make a sound. He pretended he wasn't there.

Then, suddenly, an envelope slid into the stall and came to a stop at Coke's foot.

He should have jumped up immediately and opened the stall door. He could have seen the face of the guy who slid him the note. He would have found out who was sending him all those ciphers.

Shoulda, coulda, woulda. Coke didn't open the door. Instead, he opened the envelope. It wasn't sealed. There was a sheet of white paper inside.

It was blank.

Now Coke was mad.

"Who *is* that?" he shouted, as he stuffed the paper back in the envelope and the envelope in his pocket. He got up from the toilet and reached for the little lock on the stall door.

It wouldn't open. Somehow, the stall had been locked from the outside—by the guy with the cowboy boots. And now those boots were walking across the tile floor and out of the restroom.

That's when Coke realized that he smelled

something, and it wasn't a bathroom smell. He had been in a lot of smelly bathrooms in his life, but this was worse. Much worse. It smelled like chemicals. The kind of chemicals that you're not supposed to inhale.

"I gotta get outta here," Coke mumbled to himself.

He couldn't slide under the stall door. He couldn't climb over it. He couldn't open it. He was trapped.

Gas was filling the bathroom now. There was a hissing sound, as if the gas was escaping from an aerosol container. Coke was choking, his eyes filled with tears. He couldn't call for help.

He took off his T-shirt, ripped it in half, and wrapped it around his face, hoping to filter out at least some of the poison gas. It was burning his eyes and his lungs.

He leaned on the stall door as hard as he could, but it wouldn't budge. He took a running leap at it, but the stall was too small to get enough momentum. He was starting to panic.

Finally, he just reared back and kicked the door open, like the police do on TV. The stench of poison gas filled the bathroom. Coke closed his eyes and made a mad dash for the exit door, hoping that door had not been locked too.

He stumbled out to the open air and collapsed on the grass, choking and gagging. Pep was sitting there at the picnic table, waiting for him.

"What is your problem?" she said.

"Did you get a look at the guy who just came out of the bathroom?" Coke asked her.

"Yeah, *you* just came out of the bathroom."

"I mean before me. The guy was wearing cowboy boots and a cowboy hat."

"I just got here," Pep said. "Man, what were you doing in there? I can smell it from here. What did you eat for breakfast?"

"I didn't eat anything!" Coke shouted. "Some guy tried to poison me in there! And he slipped this envelope into the stall."

"Oh, great," Pep said. "I haven't even solved the *last* cipher yet."

"I don't know if it's a cipher."

Coke took the envelope out of his pocket and showed the piece of paper to Pep.

"It's blank," she said.

"I know."

"Come on, let's get out of here before somebody sees you and thinks you caused that smell," Pep told her brother. "We can work on this in the RV."

They rushed back to the parking lot, where their parents were waiting anxiously to get back on the road.

"What happened to your shirt?" Mrs. McDonald asked Coke.

"It ripped," Coke admitted.

"We can see that," Dr. McDonald said. "How do you rip your shirt going to the bathroom?"

"Some guy in the bathroom tried to kill me with poison gas," Coke said, "so I ripped my shirt and made it into a gas mask so I could breathe."

"Ha, ha! Very funny! You kids crack me up," Dr. McDonald said. "Let's go."

"I wish you would take better care of your clothing," said Mrs. McDonald.

Dr. McDonald hit the gas and got on the highway again. In the backseat, the twins looked at the white piece of paper carefully, turning it over, holding it up to the light. It was hard enough to figure all these ciphers out when they were written clearly. Now Pep had to work from a white sheet of paper. It was frustrating.

Go to Google Maps (http://maps.google.com/).

Click Get Directions.

In the A box, type Somerset PA.

In the B box, type Williamsport MD.

Click Get Directions.

"Maybe the clue is simply 'invisible' or 'emptiness' or something like that," Coke whispered to his sister. "Or maybe the white sheet of paper is the clue itself. Maybe it means the White House! Maybe there's going to be a terrorist attack on the White House!"

"Or maybe the message was written in invisible ink," Pep guessed.

"Oh, great."

Pep put aside the white piece of paper and went back to working on the previous cipher they had received—SSGBETPLARAAENXRNDNX.

Fifteen miles down the highway, I-76 forks up toward Harrisburg and Philadelphia, and I-70 forks down toward Baltimore. Dr. McDonald merged onto I-70 South.

"I got it!" Pep suddenly exclaimed.

"What have you got, honey?" asked her mother from the front seat.

"Uh . . . poison ivy," Pep said, scratching her leg. "I think maybe I got it back at the rest station."

"We'll get some calamine lotion next time we stop."

Silently, Pep motioned for her brother to slide over next to her and look at her notebook. She had written out the cipher.

SSGBETPLARAAENXRNDNX

Then, below that, she wrote it again, but this time she divided it up into four lines.

SSGBE

TPLAR

AAENX

RNDNX

"So?" Coke asked, shrugging. "I don't get it."

"It's so simple!" Pep whispered in his ear. "I can't believe it took me so long to figure it out. Don't read it horizontally. Read it vertically."

Coke looked at the letters again.

STAR SPANGLED BANNER

"You got it!" Coke exclaimed.

"Maybe we should take her to a doctor," said Mrs. McDonald.

"I'm fine, Mom!"

Pep went back to the page in her notebook with the other ciphers on it and added the new one.

- July 3, two p.m.
- Greensboro lunch counter
- John Bull
- Star-Spangled Banner

What could it mean? What could a train, the

national anthem, and a symbol of the civil rights movement have to do with one another? Every time they got a new cipher, it made things more confusing. And now they had one that said nothing at all. Coke shook his head wearily.

Half an hour after the highway split, a sign appeared at the side of the road.

"Woo-hoo!" Coke hollered. "Did you know that the state sport of Maryland is jousting?"

"Nobody cares," Pep told him.

"Jousters care," Coke said.

They had traveled almost two hundred miles

across southwestern Pennsylvania. From the front seat, their mother informed them that they were exactly one hundred miles from Washington, D.C., now. The twins fell silent in the back of the RV. Coke didn't bother to announce any more fun facts about Maryland.

Something was going to happen in Washington. Something big.

The end was near.

Chapter 17
Y'ALL NEW TO THESE PARTS?

Soon after crossing the Maryland state line, Dr. McDonald pulled off the highway and drove a few miles to Yogi Bear's Jellystone Park Camp-Resort in Williamsport, Maryland. Mrs. McDonald checked in at the office while the kids checked out the pool. It was an uneventful night.

In the morning, Dr. McDonald said he was in the mood for poached eggs, and they didn't have any eggs in the RV. So they hit the road looking for a place that served a decent breakfast.

It wasn't long before they came upon the Blue Bell,

one of those diners that was designed to look like it was from the 1950s. There was a line of stools at the counter, silver chrome and mirrors all over the place. A big jukebox was playing "Great Balls of Fire" in the corner, alongside a glass case filled with cakes and pies that spun around slowly.

Mrs. McDonald picked up a few travel brochures from a rack on the wall. A sign said SEAT YOURSELF, so the McDonalds slid into a booth near the window. Coke was immediately absorbed in reading the menu, which was filled with Maryland trivia.

Soon the waitress, a bleached blonde wearing a pink skirt, a little pink hat, and a lot of eye makeup, came roller-skating over to the table.

"Howdy, folks," she said in a deep Southern accent. "Y'all new to these parts?"

"We're on a cross-country trip," Mrs. McDonald told her. "My sister is getting married in Washington the day after tomorrow."

"Well ain't that sweet?" said the waitress. "So what would you folks like this morning? We got eggs, bacon, sausage, muffins. . . ."

"I'll have two poached eggs on toast," said Dr. McDonald.

"Adam and Eve on a raft!" the waitress hollered to a guy in the kitchen.

"And coffee, please," added Dr. McDonald.

"Cuppa joe!" hollered the waitress.

Pep kicked Coke under the table, and he shot her a nasty glare before looking back at the menu.

"I'll have a western omelet with french fries," said Mrs. McDonald.

"One cowboy with spurs!" hollered the waitress.

"And no onions, please."

"Don't cry over it!" hollered the waitress.

"On second thought," said Mrs. McDonald, "can I get an English muffin instead of the french fries?"

"Eighty-six the spurs!" hollered the waitress. "Burn the British!"

Pep kicked Coke under the table again.

"Hey, stop it!" Coke barked at his sister.

"Stop what?" asked Mrs. McDonald.

"She's kicking me."

"Stop kicking your brother."

"I'm not kicking him."

"And how about you, little lady?" asked the waitress. "What'll ya have?"

"I'll have waffles," Pep said.

"Two checkerboards!" hollered the waitress.

"And butter, please."

"With cow paste!"

"And a glass of milk."

"One moo juice!"

"And what about you, hon?" she asked Coke.

"Do you have any cold cereal?" he asked.

"Sorry, sugar," the waitress replied. "We're fresh out."

"Then I'll have soft-boiled eggs."

"Drown the kids!" hollered the waitress.

"Do you have rye toast?" asked Coke.

"Whiskey down!"

"And a glass of orange juice too," Coke added.

"Hug one!" the waitress hollered. "Anything else?"

Dr. McDonald had been staring at the waitress ever since they came in.

"Say, haven't I met you somewhere before?" he asked. "You look familiar to me."

"'Fraid not, hon," she said. "I'm sure I woulda remembered a handsome fella like *you*."

Pep kicked Coke under the table again. When he looked at her angrily, she was mouthing the word "Mya."

Coke looked at the waitress, and she winked at him. Pep was right. Under that blond wig and all that makeup, it *was* Mya!

"I'll be back in a jiff with your grub," the waitress—that is, Mya—said.

"I gotta . . . go to the bathroom," Coke said.

"Me too," said Pep, getting up.

The twins slid out of the booth and hustled over to a hallway where the restrooms were located. Mya was waiting for them, with open arms.

"What are you doing here?" Pep asked as they hugged.

"Right now, I'm serving breakfast," she said. Her Southern accent was gone.

The short-order cook came over from the kitchen, and when he got close enough, it was obvious that it was Bones.

"How did you know we were going to stop at this diner?" Coke asked.

"We *always* know where you are," Bones replied seriously. "Listen, we need to make this quick. We've intercepted a message. Something bad is going to happen in Washington on the Fourth of July."

"That's the day after tomorrow," Mya said. "It's going to be something big."

"Are you sure it's not the *third* of July?" Pep asked.

"No, it's the fourth," Bones replied.

"Our aunt is getting married on the Fourth of July," Pep said. "We're going to be there. What's going to happen?"

"We have reason to believe there's going to be some kind of a robbery," said Bones.

"You mean somebody's going to try to steal, like, the Declaration of Independence or something?" Coke asked.

"It could be the Declaration, it could be the doorknob to the White House, or it could be the president's dog," Bones said. "It could be anything. We don't know yet. There's a lot worth stealing in Washington."

"Chances are, it will be a symbol of America," Mya added. "That's what these creeps want."

"What should we do?" Coke asked.

"Keep your eyes and ears open," Bones advised.

"You know what these people are capable of," Mya said ominously.

"They tried to kill us in Chicago, in Cleveland, and at an amusement park," Pep said. "They used poison gas on my brother at a rest stop in Pennsylvania yesterday."

"Yeah, where were *you*?" Coke asked. "We could have used your help at all those places."

"We had another mission," Bones said mysteriously. "But we'll have your back in Washington. I promise."

"Hey, where's my food?" a guy shouted in the background. "I've been waiting for half an hour."

"Comin' right up, sugar!" Mya yelled back.

"We have to go back to work," Bones said. "See you in D.C."

The twins went back to their table, where their parents were looking over the travel brochures they had picked up.

"The world's largest rubber band ball is in Chevy Chase, Maryland," Mrs. McDonald said. "It weighs over three thousand pounds, and it's fifteen feet in circumference."

"Actually, Mom, that *used to be* the world's largest rubber band ball," Coke informed her. "A guy in Southern California made one that's even bigger."

"How do you know that?" Pep asked, incredulously.

"Doesn't everybody know that?" Coke replied. "I thought it was common knowledge."

"There's a giant fiberglass pineapple in Baltimore," Mrs. McDonald said. "That could be interesting to see."

"How about we skip all that stuff and go straight to Washington this afternoon?" suggested Dr. McDonald. "I mean, which would you rather see, the Wright Brothers' first plane at the National Air and Space Museum, or a rubber band ball?"

The family debated that question for several minutes, until Mya came roller-skating back to the table carrying a big tray full of food.

"Enjoy, y'all!" she said with a wink.

Everyone dug into their breakfast. Coke tapped his egg with a spoon to crack the shell. When he peeled off the top of it, this was printed in blue on the surface of the egg:

DMOHFYNEEHN UBTELIGLPAT

"Oh no," Coke said involuntarily.

"What's the matter, dear?" asked his mother.

"Oh, uh . . . nothing," Coke replied. "I think my eggs might be hard boiled."

"We could send them back."

"Forget it."

Coke kicked Pep under the table and turned the egg slightly so she could see the letters that were printed on it. Her eyes widened.

Some ciphers take days, weeks, or even months to figure out. Others can be deciphered almost instantly by someone who knows what they're doing. Pep took one look at this one and knew the solution right away. It was simple.

She took the first letter of the first word—*D*—then the first letter of the second word—*U*. DU. Then she took the second letter of the first word—*M*—and the second letter of the second word—*B*. DUMB.

Pep looked at the egg and continued like that, remembering the letters in her head. It wasn't long before she had the whole message:

DUMBO THE FLYING ELEPHANT

"Did anybody ever hear of Dumbo the flying ele-phant?" Pep asked the family as she ate her waffles.

"*Dumbo* was an old Disney movie," Mrs. McDonald said. "Why do you ask?"

"Oh, I don't know," Pep said. "It just popped into my head."

"I never saw that movie," Dr. McDonald said, "but I seem to recall that Dumbo could fly by flapping his ears or something."

"I need to go to the bathroom," Coke said.

"Me too."

"What, again?" asked Mrs. McDonald.

The twins got up and rushed over to the bath-rooms. Pep caught Mya's eye and signaled for her to come over.

"Did you or Bones hide a secret message in my brother's egg?" Pep asked her.

"What? No, of course not. Why?"

"Somebody has been sending us these messages—John Bull, the Star-Spangled Banner, Greensboro lunch counter, and now Dumbo the flying elephant."

"Don't forget the one that said July third, two o'clock," added Coke. "That's tomorrow."

"I assure you that Bones and I have nothing to do with any of these messages," Mya said. "But all of them must tie in with each other somehow."

"What could they possibly have in common?" Pep asked her. "What could Dumbo the flying elephant possibly have in common with *anything*?"

"Somebody's playing games with you," Mya said. "But we're going to figure out who, and we're going to stop them. What concerns me is that our information says something will happen on July Fourth, and your information says July third. You kids better go back. Your parents will be suspicious."

Coke and Pep hurried back to their table and finished their breakfast quietly. When their parents went to pay the check, Coke examined his eggshell one more time. There was no writing on the shell itself.

"Hey, how is it possible to write on the *inside* of an egg without leaving a mark on the shell?" he whispered to his sister.

"It *isn't* possible," Pep told him. "But it is possible to write on the shell with special invisible ink that seeps through to the inside. It's an old trick that spies use."

"How do you know that?"

"Doesn't everybody know that?" she replied. "I thought it was common knowledge."

Dr. McDonald got back on Route 270 South and drove about thirty-three miles until he reached the exit for I-495—the capital beltway. From there, it was just eleven miles to Cherry Hill Park, a campground in College Park, Maryland.

"This is it, guys," Dr. McDonald said. "The end of the line."

"What do you mean, Dad?" Pep asked.

"We've driven all the way across the country," he told her. "We did it! Welcome to Washington, D.C.!"

"This doesn't look like Washington," Coke said, looking out the window. Some kids were playing shuffleboard.

"We're ten miles outside of the city," Mrs. McDonald explained. "It will be hard to park the RV in D.C. We'll park it here and take the Washington subway into the city."

> Go to Google Maps (http://maps.google.com/).
>
> Click Get Directions.
>
> In the A box, type Williamsport MD.
>
> In the B box, type College Park MD.
>
> Click Get Directions.

"So, we'll have all afternoon in the nation's capital," Dr. McDonald said, clapping his hands. "What do you want to see? The Washington Monument? The Air and Space Museum? Ford's Theatre? The Spy Museum?"

"The Spy Museum!" Pep shouted. "The Spy Museum!"

Chapter 18
THE SPY GUY

Cherry Hill Park is the closest—and the coolest—campground to Washington, D.C. It has two swimming pools, a hot tub, sauna, game room, miniature golf, and a playground. But after they checked in, none of the McDonalds wanted to hang around Cherry Hill Park. Everyone—and especially Pep—wanted to go into the city and spend the afternoon at the Spy Museum.

The Washington subway system is called the Metro, and the Greenbelt stop at the end of the Green line is right near Cherry Hill Park. Dr. McDonald had been to Washington many times to do research, so he knew his way around. The family took the Metro ten stops and got out when the train reached Gallery Place–Chinatown.

"This is the heart of Washington," Dr. McDonald said as they emerged from the station. They walked a short way down Seventh Street and made a right on F Street. "The White House is about seven blocks *that* way. The Capitol is about seven blocks the other way. And Ford's Theatre is right around the corner from here. That's where Abraham Lincoln was shot, you know."

"We know," said Coke, who knew just about everything, and didn't particularly enjoy hearing things he already knew.

The Spy Museum is directly across the street from the Smithsonian American Art Museum. After they paid their admission, the McDonalds were taken by elevator—along with a bunch of other people—to a little room. There, they were instructed to choose a cover identity from a bunch of choices displayed on

the walls. Just like real spies, the McDonalds had to memorize important details of their fake lives—like their names, where they were born, what they did for a living, and where they were going. After that, visitors were free to roam around the exhibits.

If you ever go to Washington, you *have* to go to the Spy Museum. It's the only public museum in the United States that is solely dedicated to espionage, and it covers the history of spying from biblical times to the present day.

There are exhibits devoted to concealment devices, sabotage weapons, intelligence gathering, audio surveillance, threat analysis, maintaining one's cover, and dead drops. A dead drop is a place—like a hole in a tree—where a spy will leave something for another spy to pick up. That's as opposed to a live drop, in which two spies will pass something—like a briefcase—from one to the other in person.

In the display cases, they have lots of cool stuff like lipstick pistols, microdots, and cameras hidden in everything from pens to buttonholes. One room is devoted to hero pigeons, which were once used to carry secret messages. Before the days of satellite surveillance, pigeons even wore tiny cameras to take photos from the sky. There is also a section devoted to famous spies who led double lives. Some of them were caught, and sometimes executed.

"Did you know that Julia Child, the French chef on TV, was a spy?" Pep asked her brother.

"Sure I did," Coke replied.

In fact, he had no idea that Julia Child was a spy. He didn't even know who Julia Child *was*. But he didn't like the idea of his sister—or anybody—knowing something he didn't.

Pep, of course, knew a lot of this already, because espionage was one of her obsessions. (The other was the Donner Party, which you would know if you read *The Genius Files: Mission Unstoppable*.) But she enjoyed seeing all this stuff with her own eyes. It was like the museum had been built just for her.

Coke and Pep were fascinated by spy paraphernalia, while their parents were more interested in cyberspying—how countries are using the internet to spy on one another and disrupt communications systems. The kids and grown-ups agreed to split up and meet in front of the museum when everybody was finished.

"Hey, check this out," Coke told his sister after his parents left, "a dog doo transmitter!"

In fact, it was for real. Inside a glass display case was a long lump of what looked to be either a Snickers bar or a dog poop. The plaque on the wall said that hidden inside it was an actual radio transmitter that the CIA used in 1970.

Toward the end of the exhibits, off in a dark corner and leaning against a fake brick wall, was a statue of a man. He was tall, dressed up in a trench coat, dark glasses, black gloves, and a hat. He was carrying a briefcase. The statue looked just like a typical spy from an old movie. The twins walked up to it.

"It looks so lifelike," Pep said. "But it's just a dummy."

Suddenly, the statue moved its hand and put it over Pep's mouth. She tried to scream, but the sound was muffled.

"Who ya calling a dummy?" the "statue" asked.

For a moment, Coke almost lost control of his bladder.

"What the—," he said instead.

"Shhhhhhhhhhh!" the guy in the trench coat said, removing his hand from Pep's mouth. "You'll blow my cover."

"Are you a spy?" Pep asked, trembling.

"Do I look like a spy?" the guy asked.

"Yes."

"Then I'm not a spy. Because if I was a spy and I looked like a spy, then I wouldn't be a very *good* spy, now would I?"

"No, I guess not," Pep said. "A good spy wouldn't look at all like a spy."

"Right, and because I look just like a spy, I couldn't possibly be one, could I?"

"No."

"But of course, if people are convinced that I'm not a spy, that would be the perfect cover for a real spy, wouldn't it?"

Coke looked at the guy closely.

"You might be a *bad* spy," he said.

"I might be. Or I might be a guy pretending to be a bad spy."

"I'm confused," said Pep.

"See these glasses I'm wearing?" the guy said. "There are cyanide pills concealed in the earpieces. If I had to, I could chew on an earpiece for a few minutes and kill myself. Glasses like these were actually used by the CIA in the 1970s."

"I bet you're just an actor who gets paid to hang around the Spy Museum answering questions about spies," said Coke.

"Maybe. Or maybe I'm a real spy *pretending* to be an actor who gets paid to hang around the Spy Museum answering questions about spies."

"Huh?" said Pep.

"Maybe I'm a spy, and maybe I'm just a guy."

"I'll call you Spy Guy," said Coke.

"Agreed."

"Whatever you are," said Pep, "can I ask you a question?"

"Shoot. I mean, go ahead."

"We received this message the other day," Pep said, pulling the white piece of paper out of her pocket, "but we don't know what it means."

Spy Guy examined the white paper, and then held it up to the light. He put his briefcase on top of a trash can and popped open the locks.

"If there's any message on this," he said, "it was written with invisible ink."

"See? I told you," Pep said to her brother.

"There are two ways of writing invisible messages," Spy Guy said. "Wet systems and transfer systems. A wet system uses ink that is only visible when it's exposed to heat or chemicals. A transfer system would use something like carbon paper."

He took a gizmo about the size of a cell phone out of his briefcase, flipped a switch, and the gizmo produced a bright purple light.

"The message is probably written in special fluorescent ink," Spy Guy said. "The ink emits visible light only when exposed to ultraviolet light of a specific wavelength."

"You really are a spy, aren't you?" Pep asked.

"Maybe. Maybe not."

Spy Guy shined the ultraviolet light over the piece of white paper, first from left to right and then from right to left. He looked at it carefully.

"So what does it say?" Coke asked impatiently.

"Nothing," Spy Guy said, turning off the light. "What we have here is a plain old white piece of paper."

"Oh no," Pep said.

Maybe her brother was right. Maybe "white paper" simply meant "White House." But what did the White House have to do with John Bull, or Dumbo the flying elephant?

"There is one other possibility," Spy Guy said, as he took a cigarette lighter out of his pocket.

"What's that?" Pep asked.

"The message could have been written with milk."

"Milk?"

"Sure," Spy Guy said. "You can make invisible ink out of milk, lemon juice, saliva, vinegar, even soapy water—anything that will oxidize when you heat it."

He flicked the lighter on and held the flame a few inches below the paper.

"Are you going to burn it?" Pep asked.

"No," Spy Guy said. "The chemical compounds in milk have a low burning point. As the paper heats up, the chemicals turn brown, but the rest of the paper stays white."

"Look!" Coke said. "It's happening!"

Slowly, lines on the paper began to darken. A few broken letters appeared, and then gradually, so did the rest of the letters. In less than thirty seconds, it was possible to read the whole message.

DOROTHY'S RUBY SLIPPERS

"That's from *The Wizard of Oz*!" Pep said excitedly. "Dorothy wore a pair of ruby red slippers, and at the end she clicked them together to go home."

Coke and Pep reviewed all the messages they had received:

- July 3, two p.m.
- Greensboro lunch counter
- John Bull
- Star-Spangled Banner
- Dumbo the flying elephant
- Dorothy's ruby slippers

The question remained, what did all those things have in common? What tied them together?

"Well, I hope that was helpful to you," Spy Guy said as he put his stuff away and closed the briefcase.

"Yes, thank you," Pep said.

"So, are you a real spy or not?" asked Coke.

"If I tell you I'm a spy, I could be a spy or I could be lying and I'm not really a spy," Spy Guy said. "And if I tell you I'm not a spy, that could be the truth or I could be lying and I'm really a spy. So it doesn't really matter how I answer that question. But I will say this. Don't believe what anybody tells you. Don't believe what you tell *yourself*. Don't believe everything you see, hear, smell or taste. Don't believe *anything*. That's my philosophy."

"Great," Coke said. "Listen, we have to go."

"Do you *really* have to go," Spy Guy said, "or are you just *saying* you have to go because you don't want to talk to me anymore?"

"Yes and no."

"Good answer."

When they finished at the Spy Museum, the McDonalds took the Metro back to the campground. Dinner was burgers and hot dogs on the grill, followed by toasted marshmallows. Afterward, Dr. and Mrs. McDonald went to see what movie was playing in the outdoor theater. Coke put on his bathing suit and went for a swim. Pep walked over to the little camp store to get a pack of gum.

After she paid the cashier, she went to look at a rack of brochures by the door. It was the usual tourist stuff—local maps, travel guides, ads for Washington bike tours and interesting attractions like the Spy Museum. Pep was about to leave when her eye was caught by a flyer on the bottom of the rack.

Pep looked at the flyer, her eyes open wide. After scanning the first two items, she gasped and almost fell over.

Discover!

HIGHLIGHTS of the
National Museum of American History

Short on time? This guide will help you find some of the things you will want to see!

Star-Spangled Banner, 1814 ▸ **2** Center
"I remember seeing my mother down on the floor, placing the stars...."
— *Caroline Purdy, daughter of Baltimore flag maker Mary Pickersgill*

Greensboro Lunch Counter, 1960 ▸ **2** East
"We decided it was really up to us to find some relief for this kind of thing we were suffering. And what started out very personal turned out to be very public."
— *Franklin Eugene McCain, one of four students who began the Greensboro sit-in*

John Bull Locomotive, 1831 ▸ **1** East
"The surprise and gratification experienced from the rapid locomotion of the engines, has been more than equaled in the current season by its wonderful capacity for propelling ponderous loads. It is a power which has almost annihilated time and space." — *From the first Annual Report of the Camden and Amboy Railroad, on the benefits of steam-powered locomotives*

Real National Treasures

Smithsonian
National Museum of American History
Kenneth E. Behring Center

americanhistory.si.edu

This guide is sponsored by the Smithsonian Women's Committee.

"You okay, miss?" the cashier asked.

"Yeah, uh, I gotta go!"

Pep grabbed one of the flyers, dashed out of the store, and went running frantically in the direction of the swimming pools to find her brother. After two laps around both of the pools, she finally found him sitting in the hot tub, his eyes closed.

"Coke! Coke!" she shouted, out of breath.

"What's the matter?"

"I know what all that stuff has in common!"

"What stuff?" Coke asked. "What are you talking about?"

"The stuff in the ciphers!" Pep said. "The Greensboro lunch counter! John Bull! The Star-Spangled Banner! And all that other stuff! I know what it all means."

"Okay," Coke said calmly, "what do they have in common?"

"They're all right here in Washington, at the National Museum of American History!"

"You gotta be kidding me!" Coke said, getting up out of the hot tub. "How do you know that?"

Pep handed him the flyer.

"And tomorrow is July third," Coke said solemnly. "We've got to be at that museum at two o'clock."

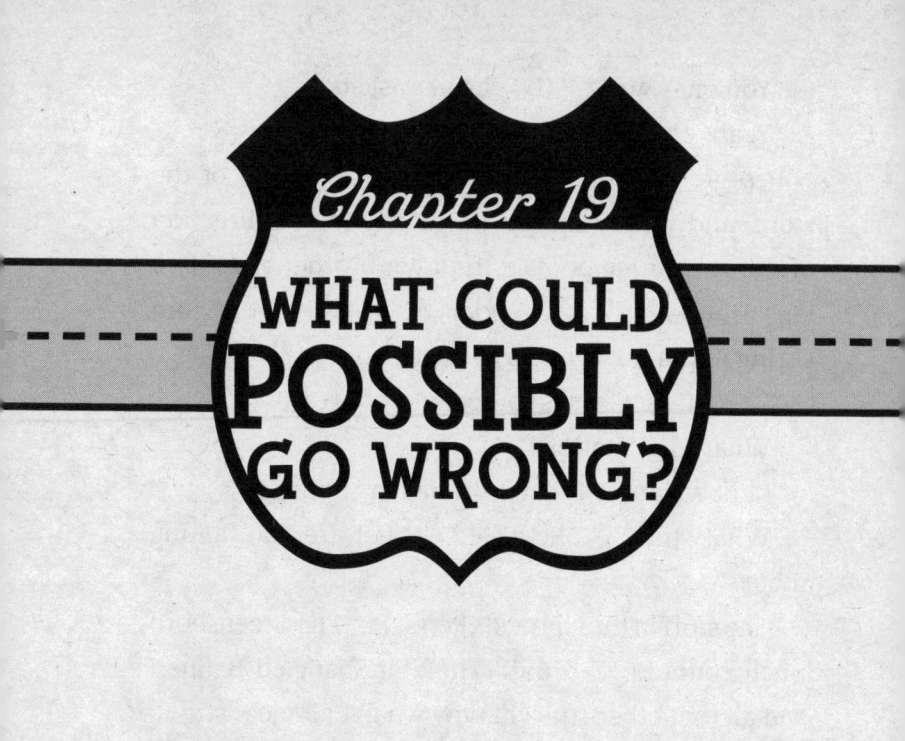

Chapter 19
WHAT COULD POSSIBLY GO WRONG?

July third. Coke and Pep enjoyed a relaxing pancake breakfast at the campground with their parents before embarking on what would turn out to be one of the most important days of their lives.

"So, we have a whole day to kill in Washington before the wedding tomorrow," Dr. McDonald announced as they cleaned the dishes. "Where shall we go? The Air and Space Museum? Museum of Natural History? Take a tour of the Capitol building? We could visit the Vietnam Memorial. . . ."

"Pep and I want to go to the Museum of American History," Coke said firmly.

"Yeah," agreed his sister.

"What? I didn't even mention *that* one."

"Why do you kids want to go there?" asked Mrs. McDonald. "How do you even know about it?"

Pep looked at Coke for guidance.

"Before school let out," Coke said, "they told us that next year the teachers are going to put a huge emphasis on social studies. So we thought going to that museum would really help us with our studies. But even more than that, it will help us learn about the history of this great land."

"Yeah," Pep agreed, "what he said."

It was a total lie, of course. Nothing had been said at school about social studies, or any other subject. But Coke knew how to blow smoke with the best of them, when he put his mind to it.

"Don't you want to go to the Museum of Natural History or the Air and Space Museum?" Dr. McDonald asked. "They have the Wright Brothers' plane there. You can see the *Spirit of St. Louis*. That's the plane Charles Lindbergh flew—"

"We know, Dad," Coke interrupted. "We've seen plenty of planes."

"Yeah, you see one plane, you've seen 'em all," added Pep.

"Ben, they want to go to the Museum of American History," said Mrs. McDonald. "That's a *good* thing. It will help them in school. You, of all people, should be supportive. You're a history teacher."

"It's just that I've visited that museum three or four times already," Dr. McDonald said, a little whiny. "I'd rather go to someplace I've never been."

Mrs. McDonald shot her husband a look, one of those looks that said he should stop being selfish and think of the children.

Coke was looking over a Washington, D.C., sight-seeing map.

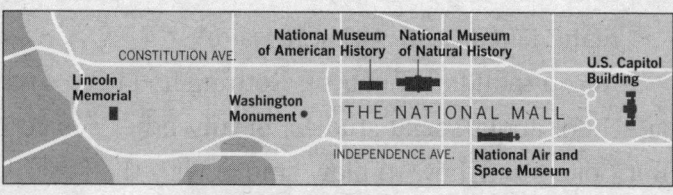

"I have an idea," he said. "The Museum of Natural History is right next door to the Museum of American History. And Air and Space is right across the National Mall. Pep and I can go to American History while you two go to one of the other museums. That way everybody will be happy."

"That's a great idea!" Pep said. "Then we can meet up when we're done."

"I don't know . . . ," Mrs. McDonald said dubiously.

"Please, Mom . . . ," Pep begged, making her best puppy dog eyes.

"Are you sure you'll be okay on your own?"

"Bridge, they're *thirteen* now," Dr. McDonald said. "They're big kids. They can handle themselves in a museum. What could possibly go wrong?"

"Yeah, what could possibly go wrong?" asked Coke, who in the last two weeks had been forced to jump off a cliff, dipped into boiling oil, drowned in ice cream, and gassed in a rest-stop bathroom.

"Well, okay. . . ."

"Yay!"

The family got a late start into Washington because Mrs. McDonald had washed some clothes and needed to wait until they were finished in the dryer before she could leave. Coke used the extra time to load up his backpack with stuff as if he was going on a commando raid. The can of Silly String he'd bought in the Miami County Museum. The duct tape they got in Avon, Ohio. The Frisbee from Bones that said TGF FLYING HIGH on it. The little bars of soap that Mya had given them at the motel. Other knickknacks he had picked up at gift shops along the road. You never know what you might need in an emergency.

They got on the Metro and rode it to Gallery Place–Chinatown again. From there, they had to switch to the red line for one stop, and then the blue line for two stops until they reached SMITHSONIAN. That stop empties out right in the middle of the National Mall, a large, grassy rectangle that is surrounded by the Smithsonian museums.

It was a glorious day. The sun was high in the sky, but it wasn't too hot. The Mall was crowded with people out walking, jogging, riding bikes, and Rollerblading.

Coke pointed out the Capitol building in the distance straight ahead, and the Washington Monument, only a block or so behind them.

The kids knew they didn't need to be at the museum until two o'clock. That was what the cipher said—July third, two o'clock. Nobody was quite ready to separate just yet. Coke pulled out his Frisbee and threw it to his dad, who threw it to his mom, who threw it to his sister, who threw it back to him. Pep was getting pretty good with a Frisbee, he had to admit. She had finally learned to throw it flat, straight, and true. After a while, they all flopped on the grass and had a little spontaneous picnic, with trail mix and snacks that always seemed to magically appear out of Mrs. McDonald's purse.

Coke had to remind himself—why were they doing this? He knew somebody or some*thing* was waiting for them inside that museum. He knew it could very well be someone who wanted to kill them. Why walk into a trap?

If he and Pep *didn't* go, he reasoned, whoever was waiting for them would come and get them. It could be tomorrow, or it could be next week or next month. But there was no avoiding it. And if he was totally honest with himself, he also had an intense curiosity to know who had been sending them all those ciphers, and what they wanted.

Coke checked his cell phone. It was one thirty.

"We should go," he told Pep.

The Museum of American History is a gigantic, blocky-looking modern building. There was a line of people waiting to get through security at the entrance. Their parents walked the twins to the end of the line and gave them a "family hug."

"You kids are getting so big, going to museums all by yourselves," Mrs. McDonald said.

"Be careful in there," warned their father. "There are pickpockets everywhere, you know."

"We'll be fine," Pep assured them. "Don't worry about us."

On the inside, she was thinking that pickpockets were the *least* of her concerns.

Mrs. McDonald pressed a twenty-dollar bill into Pep's hand and told her to go to the café in the museum if she and Coke got hungry.

"We'll stay in touch by cell phone and plan to meet

up right here when the museums close at five o'clock," Mrs. McDonald said. "Don't be late."

Don't be late.

The *late* McDonald twins. If something terrible happened, that's how people would refer to them. Coke shivered and tried to put such thoughts out of his mind.

Pep wondered if she would ever see her parents again. She tried not to cry, taking one last look at her mom and dad as they walked away.

While the twins waited on the security line, Coke played a mental video of the things that had happened to them in the last week. The incident with Archie Clone at the first McDonald's restaurant. Matching wits with Mrs. Higgins at the Cubs game in Chicago. Visiting Michael Jackson's boyhood home. Figuring out all the ciphers. Those sadistic bowler dudes. The amusement park in Sandusky, where they'd nearly drowned in ice cream. Sliding down the outside of the Rock and Roll Hall of Fame. Dad going crazy at the Hoover Historical Center when he found out that Hoover was the guy who founded the vacuum cleaner company.

He thought of the miles and miles of highway they had traveled. The strange places they'd visited. Yo-yos. Mustard. Duct tape. It had been some trip. They had traveled all the way across the United States now and seen everything from the largest egg in the world to a museum devoted to Pez dispensers. And now they were at the end of the line.

"This is it," Coke told his sister.

"Let's go," Pep replied.

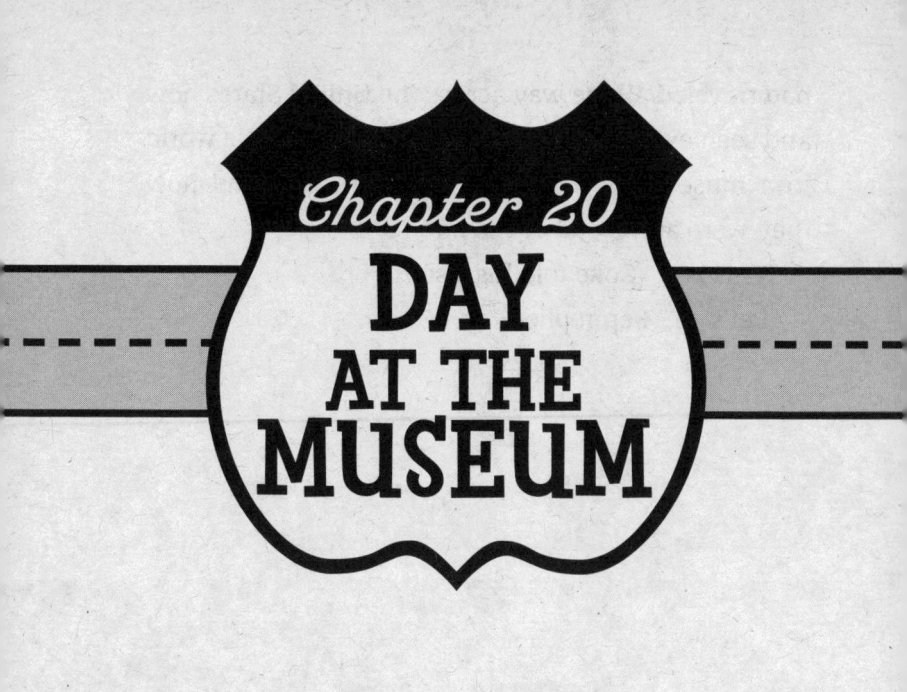

Chapter 20
DAY AT THE MUSEUM

The twins walked through the metal detector, looking all around for anything suspicious. The security guard peered into Coke's backpack for a moment, looked at Coke, rolled her eyes, and waved him through. She had seen people try to bring drugs, alcohol, explosives, and even live animals into the museum. Now *this* kid had a can of Silly String, a roll of duct tape, and little bars of soap. Nothing surprised her anymore.

There was no other line, no tickets to be picked up, no admission. The Museum of American History, like all the Smithsonian museums, is free.

Coke and Pep rushed inside. Pep checked the clock on her cell phone. It was 1:46. In fourteen minutes *something* was going to happen. The question was . . . what?

"I hope Mya and Bones show up," Coke said.

"They'll be here," Pep assured him. "They promised to have our backs."

"Look!" Coke shouted, pointing straight ahead.

On the opposite side of the museum, nearly filling the wall, was a sculpture made of hundreds of shiny silver panels arranged in the shape of a waving flag. Below it were these words:

THE STAR-SPANGLED BANNER
The Flag that Inspired the National Anthem

"This way," Coke said, marching toward it.

The entrance to the Star-Spangled Banner room was below the silver sculpture, on the right. The twins went through the doorway, not knowing what might be around the corner.

When we think of the Star-Spangled Banner, we think of the song ("*Oh say, can you see . . .*"). But the Star-Spangled Banner is a *banner*. It's the flag of the United States.

Coke and Pep walked hesitantly into a darkened

hallway with paintings on the wall and plaques describing how Francis Scott Key, on a boat a few miles from Baltimore harbor, watched ("*by the dawn's early light*") the British bombarding Baltimore's Fort McHenry on September 13, 1814. The attack lasted twenty-five hours, and explosions illuminated ("*the rockets' red glare, the bombs bursting in air*") a huge American flag, which inspired Key to write the lyrics to his famous song.

The twins turned the corner, into an even darker room. Aside from a dim line of guide lights on the floor, the only thing they could see in the room was the flag. The *real* one. The Star-Spangled Banner that had inspired Francis Scott Key. It was kept in near darkness, to prevent it from fading.

"Wow," Coke whispered. "This is the real deal."

It was the largest flag either of them had ever seen—thirty by thirty-four feet—and eight *more* feet of the right side was missing because souvenir hunters had cut off pieces over the years. One of the fifteen stars had been snipped out too. Now the flag was under glass, laid out on a tilted floor, with the lyrics to "The Star-Spangled Banner" on the wall behind it in white, glowing letters.

"Do you think somebody is supposed to meet us in here?" Pep asked. "I can't see anybody."

"I can barely see my hand in front of my face," Coke replied.

"Let's get out of here," Pep said. "It's scary."

But Coke did see one other thing in the dark room—a piece of paper on the floor in front of the display case. He stooped down to pick it up. The twins rushed out the opposite side of the dark room so they could read it. . . .

///|||||||||||||||| ||| /// ||||| // ||| || /||| ||| ||||||/||| //// ||||| ///

"Greensboro lunch counter!" Pep shouted.

They dashed out of the Star-Spangled Banner exhibit and looked to the right. Down the hall was a sculpture of George Washington wrapped in a cloth and holding one hand up in the air. They looked down the hall to the left to see . . .

A lunch counter!

"This way!" Coke said, and they ran over there.

It was a pretty ordinary-looking lunch counter, with two pink and two green stools. But history was made at that lunch counter.

It was at a Woolworth's store in Greensboro, North Carolina. Back in 1960, only white people were allowed to eat in the store. But on February 1 of that year, four black college students sat down and asked to be served. When they were told to leave, they refused. They came back the next day too, with more students from the university.

Word got around, and soon black students in fifty-four cities were holding "sit-ins" at segregated lunch counters all over the country. That drew media attention, and within six months Woolworth's and other stores had opened their lunch counters to anyone who wanted to eat there. It would be another four years until the Civil Rights Act was passed, ending segregation in public accommodations and employment.

The twins looked all over for a clue telling them what they were supposed to do or who they were supposed to see at the lunch counter. A few tourists with cameras were milling around, but they seemed harmless. Nothing really captured the twins' attention until

Coke spotted another note. This one was taped to the bottom of the glass in front of the lunch counter. He peeled it off and read it.

WBUAOHYY

"John Bull!" Pep yelled. "The train!"

They ran over to a little booth nearby with a short gray-haired lady sitting behind it. A sign next to the booth said ASK ME.

"Where's John Bull?" Pep asked breathlessly.

"Downstairs," the lady said, pointing. "When you get to the lower level, look to the right. You can't miss it."

"Thanks!" Pep said, already on the run.

"What's your rush?" the lady said. "My goodness, that old train has been sitting there for years. It's not like it's about to leave the station."

The twins thanked her and ran down the stairs. Sure enough, when they got to the bottom and looked to the right, a big, old-time train was sitting there, its smokestack almost touching the ceiling.

John Bull was one of the first steam locomotives in America. The plaque in front of it said the train was imported from England in 1831 and used to move freight and passengers between New York and Philadelphia.

Back in those days, it took two days to make that trip by horse and buggy. John Bull reduced it to five hours, which was considered amazing at the time.

But Coke and Pep weren't interested in the history of rail travel in America. They were interested in who had sent them all those ciphers and what was going to happen at two o'clock, which was now just five minutes away.

They searched all over the John Bull until Coke noticed *another* piece of paper. This one was on the tip of the big iron cow-catcher on the front of the train. He picked it off, and Pep peered over his shoulder as he looked at it.

DMOHFYNEEHN UBTELIGLPAT

"Dumbo the flying elephant!" Pep yelled first.

Directly behind the John Bull, on the wall, was a

directory of the museum's three floors. The twins searched frantically for the word "Dumbo." It wasn't there. But the directory showed a little icon on the third floor.

"That must be Dumbo!" Pep yelled.

"Follow me!" Coke said.

There was an escalator right behind the John Bull. The twins dashed up it, taking two steps at a time. They went as high as the escalator would go. At the top, they looked all around until Pep spotted a 3 WEST sign on the other side of the museum. They ran over there, and the first thing they saw, at the end of the hallway, was Dumbo.

It was part of a kiddie ride, a shiny gray fiber-glass elephant car with room for two small children to sit inside. Dumbo wore a purple hat and a white ruffled collar around his neck. The plaque in front of it said the ride had been inspired by the 1941 animated film *Dumbo*, and began operating at Disneyland soon after the park opened in 1955. Riders could make it fly up or down by moving a bar in front of them.

"Now what?" Coke asked, looking around desperately. It was 1:58. Time was running out.

There was a low glass wall surrounding Dumbo to prevent visitors from climbing on it. The twins couldn't examine Dumbo, but in the back at the bottom of the glass wall, Pep found another note.

FOLLOW DUMBO'S TRUNK

"Is it a cipher?" Coke asked.

"No!" Pep replied. "We're supposed to follow the trunk! Hurry!"

Dumbo's trunk was pointing at a slight angle to the left. There was a small gallery about twenty-five paces away, titled "Treasures of Popular Culture." Coke and Pep ran over there, and the first thing they saw in that gallery, inside a glass display case, was this:

"It's Dorothy's slippers!" Pep exclaimed. "The real ones!"

The twins pressed their noses against the glass to get a better look at the sequined shoes. The plaque explained that Judy Garland, who was just sixteen at the time, wore these sequined shoes (size five) in the movie *The Wizard of Oz*. In the original story by L. Frank Baum, Dorothy's slippers were silver. They were changed to ruby red for the movie so they would show up better against the yellow brick road.

"Well, that's all of them," Pep said, throwing up her hands. "That's all the clues."

"It's two o'clock," Coke said. "Nothing happened. Nobody's here. After all that. Maybe we made a mistake somewhere."

"Do you think it was all a big hoax?" Pep asked. "Maybe they were just playing with our heads the whole time. Nothing was going to happen on July third at two o'clock."

"Maybe Mya was right," said Coke. "Maybe it's going to happen on July Fourth."

Both of the twins were relieved, in a way. Neither of them particularly wanted to confront the unknown.

"Hey look, there's Kermit the—," Pep said, turning around to look at the rest of the exhibit.

At that moment, five guys dressed head to toe in black SWAT uniforms came running out of nowhere.

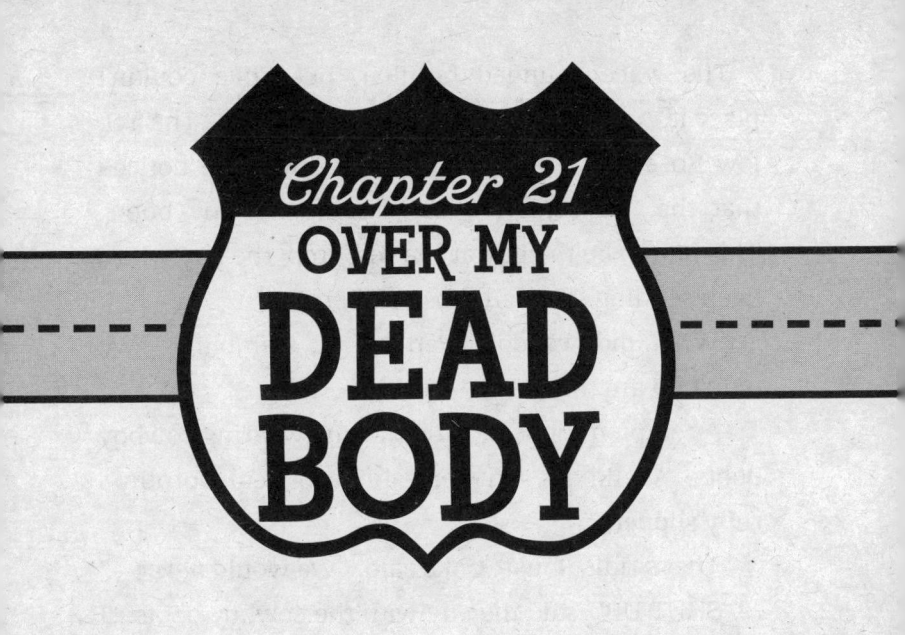

Chapter 21
OVER MY DEAD BODY

"**H**ANDS UP!"

Coke and Pep spun around to see themselves surrounded by five guys wearing black ski masks. They didn't appear to be armed, but they were all poised like ninjas, as if they were about to do martial arts moves. Three elderly tourists backed against the walls of the room, panic in their eyes.

"What?!" Coke shouted. "Who are you?"

"We're with the Washington, D.C., Police Department," one of the SWAT team barked. "You're under arrest!"

The voice sounded familiar, but Coke couldn't place it. And then the guy started whistling "The Yellow Rose of Texas." Coke looked down. He noticed that the "policeman" was wearing cowboy boots. This had to be the guy at the rest stop, the guy who'd been sending them all those ciphers.

"What did we do?" Pep asked, trembling. "We didn't do anything!"

"Attempted robbery," said the guy wearing cowboy boots. "We know you were about to steal Dorothy's ruby slippers."

"That's ridiculous!" Coke said. "We would *never—*"

"SHUT UP!" said the guy with the cowboy boots. "I don't want to hear your lame excuses. Take 'em, boys."

"Sure thing, boss," one of the SWAT team guys said, grabbing Coke roughly by the arm. Another grabbed Pep.

The three old ladies who had been looking on, shocked, now appeared to be angry.

"Kids!" one of them said, sneering. "They're a couple of juvenile delinquents."

"Imagine," the second old lady said, "stealing Dorothy's slippers. Shameful!"

"And where are their parents?" asked the third old lady. "That's the problem with children these days. No adult supervision. They just run wild in the streets."

"We didn't—," Coke tried to explain, but a black-gloved hand clapped over his mouth.

"Excuse us, folks," the guy in cowboy boots said as they made their way with the twins toward an emergency exit. "Sorry for the disturbance. Gotta keep young creeps like this off the streets. Just doing our job, you understand. Enjoy your day."

"Thank you, officers!" one of the old ladies said gratefully. "Thank you for keeping us safe."

"No problem, ma'am."

The SWAT team dragged the twins out the exit and into the dingy stairwell, locking the emergency exit door behind them. No alarms had sounded. There was no sign of Mya or Bones coming to the rescue. Coke and Pep were on their own.

There were stairs leading up from that point, presumably to the roof of the museum. Pep was trying to bite the guy holding her, but it was no use. Coke couldn't move his hands to get to any of the stuff in his backpack.

The guy wearing cowboy boots pulled off his ski mask.

"Archie Clone!" Pep said, gasping.

Yes, it was evil Archie, the lunatic who had already tried to boil the twins in oil and drown them in ice cream.

"You can take off your masks now, boys," he said. "It's safe here."

The other members of the SWAT team pulled off their masks. Coke and Pep recognized two of them as the bowler dudes who had been terrorizing them all the way across the country. The other two were pimply teenagers whose faces were not familiar. The five had posed as a legitimate SWAT team, and all of them had big, evil grins on their faces because they had pulled it off.

"It's so nice to see you two again," Archie Clone said with false sincerity. "I hope you enjoyed the museum. Did you get the chance to see Albert Einstein's pipe? Warren Harding's pajamas?"

"No, we were trying to—"

"Shut up!" Archie Clone said. "They were rhetorical questions."

"What does that mean, boss?" asked one of the bowler dudes.

"None of your business!" barked Archie Clone irritably. Then he turned back to the twins, rolling his eyes.

"Please excuse my dim-witted assistants," he whispered. "Unfortunately, I wasn't able to hire geniuses, like us. These are the guys who used to beat me up at school. Now they work for me."

"Leave us alone!" Pep shouted, trying to pull away from the bowler dude who was holding her. "You have a sickness, do you realize that? You should get help."

"Pep, Pep, Pep," Archie Clone said, shaking his head sadly. "I thought you and I had an understanding. Actually, I kinda thought you liked me. I was hoping we could watch the Fourth of July fireworks together."

"Over my dead body!" Pep shouted, causing the fake SWAT team to giggle uncontrollably.

"It's not even the Fourth of July," Coke informed Archie Clone. "That's tomorrow."

"Don't you think I know that, Coke?" Archie Clone asked. "I sent out a series of fake texts talking about a robbery in Washington on the Fourth of July. I hoped your friends Mya and Bones would intercept them. And they did. Now everyone is expecting the big robbery tomorrow. That's why I'm doing it *today*! Hahahahaha!"

"Hahahahahaha" went the fake SWAT team. They sounded like they had been programmed to laugh whenever he did.

"What are you going to steal?" Pep asked.

"Well, I could tell you, but then I'd have to kill you," said Archie Clone. "Oh, wait! I almost forgot. I'm going to kill you anyway! Hahahahaha!"

"Hahahahahaha" went the SWAT team.

"You're going to steal the Star-Spangled Banner from the museum, aren't you?" Coke guessed. "It's the symbol of America."

"Of course not," Archie Clone replied. "That's way too obvious. And besides, that flag wouldn't fit on my bedroom wall. Hahahahaha!"

"Hahahahahaha" went the fake SWAT team.

"You're going to steal Dumbo the flying elephant!" accused Pep.

"No, no, no," Archie Clone said, almost whispering, "something even *better*."

He leaned closer to Pep, so she could smell his breath. There was a gleam in his eye.

"I'm going to steal the most valuable treasure they have in this museum," he continued. "A true symbol of America. Are you ready for this? I'm going to steal . . . Abraham Lincoln's top hat!"

"No!" Coke shouted.

"You're insane!" said Pep.

"Insane?" Archie Clone said. "Seems to me that it would be insane to drive all the way across the country to see a duct tape fashion show. It's your mother who is insane."

"Leave our mother out of this!" Pep shouted.

"Oh, please," said Archie Clone. "Spare me the theatrics."

"How about we just kill 'em now, boss?" asked one of the bowler dudes. "Right here in the stairwell."

"Not yet," Archie Clone said. "Not here."

He pulled a photo out of his pocket and showed it to the twins.

"As you know, I have a . . . thing . . . for hats," he told them. "This one was made by J. Y. Davis, a Washington hatmaker. Lincoln had the black silk mourning band added in honor of his son, Willie, who got sick and died at the age of eleven. And do you know when Lincoln wore this hat for the last time?"

"When?" Pep asked.

"April fourteenth, 1865," Archie Clone said, "on his way to Ford's Theatre."

"The night he was shot," Coke said.

"That's right," said Archie Clone. "After the assassination, the hat was given to the Patent Office, and they transferred it to the Smithsonian Institution in 1867. The hat was stashed in a basement storage room for twenty-six years. After they put it on display, it became one of the most treasured objects in the museum. And soon it will be part of my unique hat collection! Hahahaha!"

"Hahahahahaha" went the fake SWAT team.

"I thought all you cared about was getting Dr. Warsaw's million dollars for being the last surviving member of The Genius Files," Coke said.

"A million dollars?" Archie Clone said with a snort. "That's petty cash! Do you have any idea how much Lincoln's top hat would be worth?"

"It doesn't matter," Pep said. "As soon as you try to sell it, you'll get caught. Nobody would buy it from you. They'd know it was stolen from the museum."

"All very true, Pep," Archie Clone said, looking at his watch, "but I can ransom it, and for a lot more than a million dollars. My good friend Mrs. Higgins is downstairs stealing the top hat right now, as we speak."

"So you and Mrs. Higgins *are* working together!" Pep said.

"She'll never get away with it," Coke said. "It's under glass. There are security guards."

"Hahahahahaha" went the fake SWAT team.

"Glass? Security guards?" Archie Clone said. "You must be joking, Coke. Take them upstairs, boys."

The fake SWAT team shoved Coke and Pep up the stairs to the next level. There were no more stairs above that. A gray door had three words stenciled on it in black—MUSEUM ROOF ACCESS.

Coke and Pep stopped instinctively. Roofs are dangerous places. They're high, for one thing. People fall off them, for another. And die.

"What do *we* have to do with Abraham Lincoln's hat?" Pep asked. "Why don't you just steal it and leave us alone?"

"I'm glad you brought that up, Pep," said Archie Clone. "I've been keeping an eye on you two for a long time. Dr. Warsaw tried to kill you on several occasions, but he failed. After he died and I took over The Genius Files program, I dipped you in boiling oil, but you somehow managed to escape. I tried to drown you in ice cream, but you escaped again. That impressed me. I like your style. You two almost seem . . . unkillable, if that's a word."

Coke said a few words to Archie Clone that you have undoubtedly heard on the playground or perhaps even when your parents are really, really mad. Needless to say, they are not nice words.

"I'll disregard that remark," Archie Clone said. "Because I could really use a couple of resourceful kids like you in my operation. Geniuses, so to speak. It would be a big improvement over the current personnel, if you know what I mean."

"We're not geniuses," Pep said. "Never say genius again!"

"I'm going to give you kids a choice," Archie Clone said. "Join me. I'll cut you in on whatever I do. We'll be equal partners. Stick with me, and we're going to have a lot of fun and make a lot of money. You'll be set for life. This is a golden opportunity for you."

"What's our other choice?" Coke asked.

"Your other choice?" Archie Clone said. "Well, your other choice, of course . . . is to *die*."

"We would *never* work for you!" Pep said, almost spitting out the words in his face. "Not if our lives depended on it."

"That's too bad," Archie Clone said, "because your lives *do* depend on it. Take them up to the roof, fellows. Maybe they'll change their tune once we get up there."

One of the bowler dudes pushed open the roof access door, and Coke and Pep were shoved through it.

They were outside now. From this height, the Washington Monument appeared to be very close, almost looming over them.

There were three helicopters parked on the roof. Nobody was inside them, but their rotors were turning slowly. One of the bowler dudes shoved the twins toward the nearest chopper.

"Did you know that when the president of the United States travels by helicopter, there are always three identical helicopters in the air?" Archie Clone said. "That way, if somebody wanted to shoot his helicopter down, they won't know which one to shoot at. It also means that if there are three helicopters flying around Washington, the police don't bother them because they assume the president is inside one of them. Get in."

Coke and Pep didn't have any choice. The bowler dude pushed them into the helicopter, and Archie Clone climbed into the pilot's seat.

"Where is Mrs. Higgins with my top hat?" he asked nobody in particular. "What's taking her so long? She probably stopped to wash her hands or some such nonsense."

"Where are you taking us?" Pep demanded.

"Not far," Archie Clone replied. "If you don't want to join my team, I'll drop you two off at the Washington Monument."

"You mean you're going to let us go after you steal Lincoln's hat?" asked Pep hopefully.

"No," Archie Clone said as he fiddled with the controls. "I said I'd drop you off at the Washington Monument. The key word is *drop*. I can't have you two blabbing about my plans."

"You're going to drop us *on* the Washington Monument?" Pep asked.

"It's a beautiful structure, isn't it?" Archie Clone said as he gazed skyward. "Looks like a gigantic, sharpened pencil. Most people don't know this, but there's an aluminum cap at the top, with eight lightning rods attached to it. Each of them are six inches long. Get the point?"

"You're a lunatic!" Coke shouted.

"I know, I know," Archie Clone said. "It won't be easy to drop you two right on the point. But if I miss by a few inches, it's okay. You'll fall 555 feet, 5 and

1/8 inches to the ground. The impact will finish the job. So it's a win-win for me."

He pushed a button on the dashboard, and the helicopter's rotors started spinning faster. The bowler dudes ran over and climbed into the other two helicopters.

Pep was paralyzed with fear. She gripped the seat tightly, as if that would somehow protect her. In his head, Coke frantically calculated their options. He and Pep could jump out and make a run for it. They could try to overpower Archie Clone. Or they could just sit there and hope somebody would rescue them. He looked up at the Washington Monument. Once the chopper was up in the air, all bets were off.

Archie Clone pulled out a cell phone.

"Hurry up, Higgins!" he barked once he'd made the connection. "What's taking so long? I haven't got all day. I want my top hat, and I want it *now*!"

While Archie Clone was talking, Coke leaned over to his sister.

"When I say so, we're going to jump out," he whispered in her ear.

"I can't!" she whispered back. "We might get killed!"

"We're sure to get killed if we *don't* jump out," Coke said. "Come on. Just like we jumped off the cliff. You've got to trust me."

Archie Clone cursed and slapped his cell phone shut. He saw something in the distance that the twins didn't—another helicopter coming from across the National Mall. He flipped a few switches, and the rotors spun faster.

"Where is Higgins?" Archie Clone said, looking around angrily. And then, "That's it, forget the stupid hat. I'm getting out of here."

Coke saw the helicopter approaching too.

"Look! I'll bet it's the real cops!" he shouted. "You might as well surrender. You're done for."

"Not if I can help it," Archie Clone said.

He pulled back on the joystick, and the helicopter began to lift off the roof.

As the other helicopter got closer, Coke could see that there were no policemen in it.

"It's Mya and Bones!" he shouted, pointing.

"Not *them*!" Archie Clone spat.

"I told you they'd be here!" shouted Pep.

The helicopter the twins were in was five feet above the roof.

"We've got to jump *now*!"

"I can't!"

As the other helicopter reached the roof, Mya jumped out. She had a bag around her neck. She reached into the bag and pulled out an orange Frisbee.

"It's a Frisbee grenade!" Coke yelled. "She can't see us! She's going to blow us up!"

Their helicopter was almost ten feet above the roof now. Coke couldn't wait any longer. He gave Pep a shove and pushed her out. Then he jumped out himself, landing clumsily on the roof next to his sister and twisting his ankle painfully.

Mya got into position to throw the Frisbee at Archie Clone's chopper. She was about to let it loose when—

Fttttttttttttttttttttttttt!

A dart hit Mya on the side of her neck! Coke looked to the right and saw one of the bowler dudes sitting in a chopper with a blowgun in his mouth. Then that chopper flew away.

Mya stopped, her eyes rolling back in her head. She crumpled to her knees, dropping the Frisbee.

It was like everything was in slow motion as the Frisbee fell to the concrete. Coke put his hands on his ears in anticipation of the inevitable explosion.

But nothing happened. There was no explosion.

"The Frisbee detonates on the *second* impact!" Pep shouted. "Remember? She skips it off the ground!"

Pep ran over and grabbed the Frisbee. Archie Clone's chopper was about fifteen feet off the roof now, and moving horizontally. In a few seconds, it would be out of range.

"Throw it!" Coke shouted to his sister.

"He's leaving!" Pep shouted back. "I can't—"

At that moment, Archie Clone stopped his helicopter and swiveled it around.

"You kids think you are so smart," he shouted out the open window. "Well, *nobody* is smarter than me."

He pulled out what appeared to be a gun but was in fact much worse than a gun. It was a missile launcher, the kind that terrorists use. One well-placed shot could take off the roof of the museum. Archie Clone pointed the monstrous thing at the twins and looked through the scope.

"Throw it, Pep!" Coke shouted. "Now!"

Pep reared back and whipped the Frisbee hard, so hard that she fell down as she let fly. The Frisbee hit the chopper just above the fuel tank. A moment later there was a flash, followed by a fireball that enveloped the whole chopper. I'm talking about a big, orange, action-movie fireball.

Coke covered his eyes to shield himself from the flash of light, the heat, and the flying debris.

"Nice throw!" he said, genuinely impressed by his sister's skill.

The flaming chopper spun crazily for a few seconds, and then crashed into the ground next to the museum, resulting in another fireball. Terrified tourists scattered to avoid getting hit.

Coke and Pep looked over the edge of the roof to watch the twisted wreckage smoke and burn. Nobody climbed out of the chopper. There would be no survivors.

Pep began to sob. Her brother put his arm around her.

"I killed somebody," she said quietly.

"We *both* killed him," Coke told her. "There was no other way."

Bones landed his chopper on the roof, jumped out, and ran over to the twins.

"Get out of here!" he implored them. "Quick, before the police show up to find out what happened."

By five o'clock, when the museums closed for the day, teams of very official-looking workers had carted away most of what was left of the burned helicopter outside the Museum of American History. There had been a story on the news about a helicopter crash near the Washington Monument, but government officials had managed to keep the details of the accident away from the press. Life had returned to normal on the National Mall. People were jogging and skateboarding as if nothing had ever happened.

Coke and Pep were lying around on the grass when their parents came strolling out of the National Air and Space Museum.

"So did you kids have a good time?" asked Dr. McDonald. "Did you see Albert Einstein's pipe?"

"How about Warren Harding's pajamas?" asked Mrs. McDonald.

"It was really cool," Coke told them. "We saw the actual flag that inspired Francis Scott Key to write 'The Star-Spangled Banner.'"

"And we saw that John Bull train. Did you know it used to take two days to get from New York to Philadelphia?"

"And Dumbo the flying elephant . . ."

"And Dorothy's ruby slippers from *The Wizard of Oz* . . ."

"We learned a lot about American history," Coke told his parents. "I think it's going to really help us in school this year."

"Great!" Dr. McDonald said. "I'm so glad you kids went there. See? It's possible to go places that are fun and educational at the same time."

"You're limping, Coke," Mrs. McDonald said. "What happened?"

Coke looked at his sister.

"Well, the truth is," he said, "we were kidnapped by this crazy teenager who looked like Archie from the comics. He dragged us up to the roof of the museum, where he was going to take us by helicopter and drop us on the point of the Washington Monument. But we jumped out at the last moment and Pep threw a Frisbee grenade at the chopper and blew it out of the sky. I twisted my ankle when I jumped out of the helicopter."

Their parents looked at him for a long time.

"Ha, ha!" laughed Dr. McDonald. "That's a good one. You kids crack me up."

"Hey," Mrs. McDonald said. "What do you say we go watch some fireworks tonight? Tomorrow is the Fourth of July, you know."

"I don't think so, Mom," Pep said. "It's been a long day."

Chapter 22
TILL DEATH DO YOU PART

Coke and Pep's long nightmare was finally over. Archie Clone was dead, a victim of his own greed and insanity. Dr. Warsaw was dead, a victim of a very high fall from The Infinity Room at The House on the Rock. Mrs. Higgins was, in all probability, in police custody, after foolishly trying to steal the top hat that Abraham Lincoln was wearing on the night he was assassinated. The bowler dudes had flown away in helicopters, but neither of them seemed to have the smarts to mount a serious campaign of terror without the guidance of an inspiring leader.

There was nobody left to bother Coke and Pep. When they woke up on the morning of July Fourth, they were both smiling for the first time in a long time. A burden had been lifted. Finally, they could enjoy their summer vacation.

Everyone rushed to get dressed. Aunt Judy's wedding was scheduled for noon on the grass in front of the Lincoln Memorial. The McDonald family had packed their nicest clothes for this occasion, and had waited the whole trip to wear them.

Before this year, Pep had never cared much about clothes or what she looked like. But today she was all decked out in a lovely blue skirt with a ruffled white blouse and a necklace with a butterfly on it. Coke hated to wear a jacket and tie, and put up with them as long as it was just for the occasional wedding or funeral. His pants and sleeves were just a *little* short, because he had grown a few inches in the last year but had refused to go shopping to get new clothes that fit. Dr. McDonald had on the jacket he wore to work every day, with a red, white, and blue tie. Mrs. McDonald wore a conservative flower print skirt. She didn't want to put on anything that might outshine her sister, the bride and star of the show.

Everyone in the McDonald family was used to throwing on a pair of shorts and a T-shirt in the morning. So getting ready took longer this day, fussing with all the ties and buttons and zippers and belts. But in the end, they looked good. The all-American family. People stared at them as they boarded the Metro heading into Washington.

The Fourth of July is a special day. It's America's birthday, after all, and everyone wants to go to the party in the nation's capital. People were holding little flags. Red, white, and blue was everywhere.

Mrs. McDonald was understandably nervous about the wedding. She had not seen her sister, Judy, in many years. Bridget and Judy had grown up together in California, but after college Judy had moved to Washington to take an entry-level job in the government. For a short time, she worked at the Pentagon. Bridget and Judy had a falling-out when Judy started going out with—and almost married—a boy that Bridget didn't like. He seemed mean and abusive, and she didn't want her sister mixed up with a guy like that. Judy broke up with the boy a long time ago, but she and Bridget didn't reconnect after that. They had stopped speaking, and neither one wanted to be the first to apologize. Bridget was surprised when she received an invitation to Judy's wedding. Maybe it was a signal that their feud was over.

In any case, the sisters hadn't seen each other in ten years. Coke and Pep didn't remember meeting their Aunt Judy when they were very little.

The McDonalds were already running late for the

wedding, and there was a delay on the Metro that made them even later. They got out at the Foggy Bottom Metro stop and rushed about half a mile toward Potomac Park, where the Lincoln Memorial is located.

"I barely remember what Judy looks like anymore," Mrs. McDonald said as they hurried down Twenty-third Street.

"She probably looks the same," said Dr. McDonald. "Just a little older and grayer. Like us."

"What should I say to her?"

"Just say congratulations."

"What if she's marrying some jerk?"

"That's her business, not yours," Dr. McDonald advised. "Don't judge her. That's what caused all the problems last time. Besides, how bad could he be?"

It was a beautiful day, and lots of tourists were out. The McDonalds were looking for people dressed as a bride and groom.

"Over there!" Coke said as they crossed Constitution Avenue.

Hundreds of folding chairs had been set up in front of the Lincoln Memorial. The McDonalds grabbed the only four consecutive seats that were empty, in the back. They could barely see the big statue of Abraham Lincoln. It looked like they had arrived just in time. The bride had already walked down the aisle, but the ceremony had not started yet. The Elvis

Presley song "Love Me Tender" was playing out of a big set of speakers.

Dr. McDonald took some coins out of his pocket and handed Coke a penny.

"Notice anything familiar?" he asked.

Coke looked at the penny and turned it over. The image on the back was exactly what he was looking at—the Lincoln Memorial.

"You know," Dr. McDonald said, "this is the spot where Martin Luther King Jr. gave his 'I Have a Dream' speech."

"I know, I know," Coke said.

"Isn't this beautiful?" Mrs. McDonald asked, to nobody in particular, as she fussed with her hair.

"I wonder how they were able to get a permit for this space," Dr. McDonald commented. "Somebody must have a lot of dough, or a lot of clout."

"Shhhhh, you're spoiling the mood, Ben."

"All I'm saying is, you can't just pay somebody a hundred bucks to rent the Lincoln Memorial. Somebody pulled some strings—"

"Shhhhhhhhhhh!"

"Mom," Pep complained, "I can only see the backs of their heads from here."

"Shhhhhhhhhhh! We'll talk to Aunt Judy and her new husband after the ceremony."

Mrs. McDonald stood up for a moment to get a better look at the front. She couldn't see much. The bride was wearing a traditional long white gown. The minister was standing at a podium, fussing with some papers. The groom appeared to be sitting in a wheelchair.

"I didn't know Judy's fiancé was disabled," she said.

"Shhhhhhhhhh!" Dr. McDonald replied. "I think they're about to start."

Mrs. McDonald sat back down. The buzzing in the crowd fell to a hush as the minister began to speak.

"Dearly beloved," he said, "we are gathered together here to join together this man and this woman in holy matrimony. . . ."

Coke looked around. He wished he'd brought a portable video game system, or his iPod. This was going to be boring.

"Marriage is the joyous joining of two people in heart, in body, and in mind," the minister continued. "In marriage, two people make a lifelong commitment to embrace their dreams, to face their failures, their disappointments, and to one day realize their hopes together."

Mrs. McDonald started to tear up, and Dr. McDonald handed her a tissue. Coke looked around to see tissues being passed around among the sniffling crowd. Even Pep looked like she was getting a little choked up.

Coke looked over at his dad, and they winked at each other as if to share a secret—*Weddings are a girl thing*. It would be so much more fun if he and all the guys at the wedding could go to a ball game instead. Probably even the groom would come along.

"This occasion is a celebration," the minister continued. "A celebration of the love and commitment with which this man and this woman begin the rest of their lives together. We are here today to witness their joining in marriage, one of the holiest bonds."

Coke looked around. The stupid tie was choking his neck. Some of the men weren't wearing ties. Why did he have to? One guy even had shorts on.

He noticed that the Washington Monument was directly behind them, about a mile in the distance. He thought about what might have happened if things had gone differently there the day before. He wondered which was worse, being dropped from a helicopter onto the tip of the Washington Monument, or having to sit through a wedding ceremony.

"What greater thing is there," the minister continued, "than for two souls to be joined together in love, loyalty, trust, and honesty? In marriage, two people promise each other to aspire to these ideals throughout their lives, because with mutual understanding, openness, sensitivity, care, respect, responsibility, and knowledge comes the appreciation of one's own happiness, growth, and freedom."

Coke had barely heard anything the guy said after "Dearly beloved." The words just washed over him. He checked his cell phone for the time, looked around some more, and wondered when it was going to be over.

The minister continued.

"If any person can show just cause why this man and this woman may not be joined together in holy matrimony, let them speak now or forever hold their peace."

Coke looked around again. In the movies, this was the part where some old boyfriend would always jump up, tell the bride he still loved her, and the two of them would go run off together, leaving the groom and everybody else staring with their mouths open. No such luck this time. Everyone looked around at one another for an awkward moment or two, and then the minister turned to face the bride and continued.

"Do you, Judy McAllister, take this man to be your husband in the holy state of matrimony? Will you love him, comfort him, honor and keep him, in sickness and in health, for richer, for poorer, for better, for worse, in sadness and in joy, as long as you both shall live?"

"I will," Aunt Judy said.

The minister smiled and turned to face the groom, sitting in his wheelchair.

"And do you, Herman Warsaw—"

EPILOGUE

What?! Are you kidding me? Dr. Warsaw is *alive*? He wasn't supposed to have survived the fall from The Infinity Room! His obituary was in the newspaper! How could he possibly still be alive?

What happened to Mrs. Higgins? Where did the bowler dudes fly off to? And what would it be like to have your mother's sister married to a psychotic mass murderer who was trying to kill you?

To find out the answers to these and other questions, well, you'll just have to read *The Genius Files #3*.

I'll tell you one thing right now, though.

It's going to be a long ride back to California.

ABOUT THE PHOTOS

In The Genius Files, Coke and Pepsi McDonald take a cross-country trip, and I thought it would be cool to use photos of road signs to mark their progress. I was not in a position to go cross-country myself or to pay professional photographers to shoot the signs for me, but I have many loyal readers on my Facebook fan page, and they're scattered all over the country. So I put out the word that I needed photos of some specific road signs, and instantly people came through for me. They shot all the photos I needed.

Thank you to these fans, and to the Hoover Historical Center, for providing me with these photos:

Page 21, Amanda LeBrun

Page 23, Kelly Salgado

Page 81, Katie Jergensen

Page 91, Liat Shapiro

Page 94, Mary Kittrell

Page 121, Tony Packo's Inc.

Page 186, Hoover Historical Center / Walsh University, North Canton, Ohio

Page 194, Jabin Mallory

Page 207, Ellie Goldenberg

ABOUT THE AUTHOR

Dan Gutman is the author of such immensely popular books as *Honus & Me*, *The Homework Machine*, *The Kid Who Ran for President*, *The Million Dollar Shot*, and the My Weird School series. If you'd like to find out about Dan and how he got started as a writer, you can visit him online at www.dangutman.com.

The most dangerous
road trip in history continues!

Turn the page for a sneak peek at the third
action-packed book in The Genius Files series.

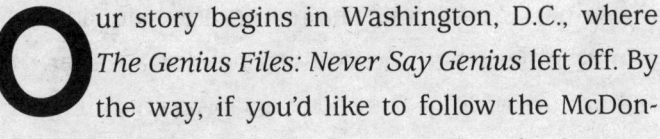

UNCLE
HERMAN

Our story begins in Washington, D.C., where *The Genius Files: Never Say Genius* left off. By the way, if you'd like to follow the McDonalds on their journey, it's easy. Get on the internet and go to Google Maps (http://maps.google.com/), Mapquest (www.mapquest.com), Rand McNally (www.randmcnally.com), or whatever navigation website you like best.

Go ahead, I'll wait.

Okay, now type in Lincoln Memorial, Washington, D.C., and click SEARCH MAPS. Click the little + or – sign on the screen to zoom in or out until you get a sense of where the twins are. See it? That's our starting point.

It was July 4th, a beautiful sun-drenched afternoon in the nation's capital. The temperature outside was almost ninety, but you couldn't ask for a better day to have a wedding. The sad eyes of Abraham Lincoln looked down over the one hundred or so guests.

"Do you, Judy McAllister, take this man to be your husband in the holy state of matrimony? Will you love him, comfort him, honor and keep him, in sickness and in health, for richer, for poorer, for better, for worse, in sadness and in joy, as long as you both shall live?"

"I will," Aunt Judy said quietly.

Coke turned to look at his mother, who was

beaming. She and Judy, her little sister, had not always gotten along while they were growing up. But all was forgiven now.

The minister turned to face the groom, who was sitting in a wheelchair.

"And do you, Herman Warsaw, take this woman to be your wife in the holy state of matrimony? Will you love her, comfort her, honor and keep her, in sickness and in health, for richer, for poorer, for better, for worse, in sadness and in joy, as long as you both shall live?"

"I do."

"By the power vested in me by the District of Columbia, I pronounce you husband and wife. You may kiss the bride."

For a moment or two, Coke and Pep didn't quite grasp what they had just heard. Did that minister really say "Herman Warsaw"?

It couldn't be! Dr. Warsaw was dead. Coke had personally karate kicked him out of The Infinity Room back in Wisconsin a week earlier. It had been hundreds of feet up in the air. There was no way he could have survived the fall. And besides, they had seen Dr. Warsaw's obituary in the newspaper. Maybe this guy was a different Herman Warsaw.

But no, there he was, sitting in a wheelchair.

All decked out in a tuxedo.

And getting married.

Kissing.

Aunt Judy.

As smart as they were, it took another moment or two for Coke and Pep to fully process the information. Dr. Warsaw was the reason they had been forced to jump off a cliff near their home in California. He was the reason they were locked in a burning school, pushed into a sand pit, and nearly drowned in a vat of bubbling Spam. It was because of him that they were zapped with electric shocks, lowered into boiling oil, and chased through the streets of Chicago. If Aunt Judy was their mother's sister, and she was marrying Dr. Warsaw, then that meant that Dr. Warsaw was now . . .

Uncle Herman!

They were related! Dr. Warsaw would be part of their family! How do you sit around the table on Thanksgiving with the man who tried to kill you?

Pep's jaw dropped open, and the blood drained from her face.

"Are you okay, sweetie?" asked her father. "You're white as a ghost."

That's when Pep's eyes rolled back in her head, and she collapsed.

NOW IT'S PERSONAL

We need a doctor over here!"

People were hollering for help before Pep had even hit the ground.

She was unconscious, lying on the grass, for about thirty seconds. When she opened her eyes, a doctor was leaning over her—Dr. Herman Warsaw.

Women, for unexplained reasons, found him irresistible. He was an odd-looking man. Extremely thin and squinty eyed, Dr. Warsaw was a chain smoker who dressed in baggy suits that made it look like he belonged in an old gangster movie. Years before, he had been a brilliant inventor who made a fortune with a GPS for people to track down their lost pets. A millionaire many times over, he got bored with making money and turned his attention to solving society's problems by enlisting the young people of the world. Then, of course, came 9/11, when the seeds of his insanity were germinated.

"She'll be okay," Dr. Warsaw proclaimed. "The heat must have gotten to her. She just needs a little air."

He had actually climbed down from his wheelchair to sit on the grass next to Pep. Somebody handed him a water bottle, and he put it to her lips, cradling her head in his arms like she was an injured puppy.

"What an adorable young lady," he said.

Pep, too petrified to move or speak, just stared at him, eyes wide-open. Coke watched from a few feet away, dumbfounded, as his sister was being nursed back to health by the man who had repeatedly tried to murder them.

Dr. Warsaw seemed to have matters well in hand, so the other grown-ups drifted away into small groups to do what grown-ups love to do—make small talk. Catch up. Introduce each other. Discuss the weather, as if it mattered. Mrs. McDonald ran over to hug Aunt Judy and congratulate her.

When the other grown-ups had become sufficiently

distracted, Dr. Warsaw lowered his voice so only the twins could hear.

"So we meet again," he whispered, his voice dripping with hatred. "I should just choke your sister to death right now, Coke."

"And I should just throw you on that wheelchair and push it down the steps," Coke said, "but that wouldn't look very good in front of all the relatives."

"I never expected you two to make it this far," Dr. Warsaw said quietly. "I thought I had gotten rid of you back in Cleveland at the Rock and Roll Hall of Fame. I'll say one thing about you brats. You are quite resourceful."

"And I thought *you* were dead at The House on the Rock after we pushed you out of The Infinity Room," Pep croaked.

"I almost was, thanks to you little punks!" Dr. Warsaw whispered. "Just about every bone in my body broke when I hit the ground. The doctors say I may never walk again."

"Boo-hoo," Coke said sarcastically.

"We were just defending ourselves!" Pep protested. "You were trying to kill *us*."

"Yes, and after that you killed my protégé, Archie. I spent years training that fine young man to carry on with my work. He was the son I never had."

Tears welled up in Dr. Warsaw's eyes as he talked about Archie Clone.

"He was trying to kill us too!" Pep pointed out. "He was going to drop us on the tip of the Washington Monument!"

"Oh, it's always about *you*, isn't it?" Dr. Warsaw sputtered, his face clenched. "Well, listen to me, you spoiled brats, and listen good. The differences between us have nothing to do with The Genius Files program anymore. Now it's personal."

"Wh-what are you gonna do to us?" Pep asked.

"Right now, sadly, I am in no condition to do anything to you," Dr. Warsaw told them. "But these broken bones will heal soon enough. And when they do, I'm going to track you down like dogs and make you pay for what you did to me and my young friend Archie. Believe me, you're going to wish you never tangled with me."

"We *already* wish we never tangled with you," Pep said. "You started it!"

"Don't argue with him," Coke told his sister, "He's insane!"

"Perhaps," Dr. Warsaw said. "Insanity and genius often go hand in hand."

"Let's blow this pop stand," Pep said as she stood up and brushed the grass off her dress.

Dr. Warsaw grabbed her wrist roughly before she could get away.

"Oh, and by the way," he said, "if you say one word about any of this to your parents, I will kill them both. I don't care if we're all related now. Mark my words. You know I do not make idle threats."

The other grown-ups, having run out of small talk, straggled back to get their belongings and say their good-byes. Mrs. McDonald and Aunt Judy were arm in arm, reminiscing about their childhoods.

"I'm so glad the whole family was able to be here for our special day!" said Aunt Judy.

"We wouldn't have missed it for the world," replied Mrs. McDonald. "You two seem so happy together."

"It was love at first sight," Aunt Judy gushed. "The second I set eyes on Hermy, I knew I had met the kindest, sweetest, most wonderful man in the world."

"You are *too* kind, my love," said Dr. Warsaw as he pulled himself back onto the wheelchair.

"Hermy?" asked Coke.

Pep looked like she might pass out again.

"You okay, Pep?" asked her father.

"I'll survive," she said.

Dr. Warsaw let out a nervous laugh.

"I'm glad you had the chance to meet our children," said Mrs. McDonald. "Now that you and I are family and everything."

"Yeah, family," muttered Coke. "One big, happy family."

"You have two lovely children," Dr. Warsaw said, pinching Pep's cheek just a little harder than necessary. "We had a nice chat just now. I look forward to getting together again very soon."

"Maybe after our honeymoon is over," added Aunt Judy. "We're going to California."

"Well, that's perfect!" said Dr. McDonald. "So are we!"

After lots of hugs and kisses all around, Aunt Judy wheeled Dr. Warsaw over to a van that had been specially outfitted with a wheelchair lift. She helped him inside. A dozen cans had been tied with string to the rear bumper and the words JUST MARRIED were written on the back window. All the guests gathered around to wave their good-byes and good wishes to the happy couple while the strains of Elvis Presley's "Love Me Tender" played in the background.

As Aunt Judy was starting up the van, Dr. Warsaw turned his head to make eye contact one last time with Coke and Pep. And as the van was pulling away, he glared at them with the evil eye.